CLIFF'S EDGE

Cliff's Edge

Carolyn Hart

All rights reserved, including without limitation the right to reproduce this book or any portion thereof in any form or by any means, whether electronic or mechanical, now known or hereinafter invented, without the express written permission of the publisher.

This is a work of fiction. Names, characters, places, events, and incidents either are the product of the author's imagination or are used fictitiously. Any resemblance to actual persons, living or dead, businesses, companies, events, or locales is entirely coincidental.

Copyright © 2014 by Carolyn Hart

ISBN: 979-8-3372-0444-4

This edition published in 2026 by Open Road Integrated Media, Inc.
180 Maiden Lane
New York, NY 10038
www.openroadmedia.com

*To Deborah Adams, friend, editor, and fellow writer.
Thank you for your generosity, humor, and kindness.
And for taking a gamble on a suspense novel set in
first-century Rome!*

CLIFF'S EDGE

I

He stood naked on the rocky bluff, poised to dive down into the darkening blue water of the secluded cove. His body glistened in the amber wash of the late afternoon sun, magnificent as a bronze charioteer.

Camilla knew she should turn away, but his beauty held her captive as it had since she'd first seen him across the narrow chasm a few weeks ago. She'd returned to the cliff's edge every evening since that first glimpse. Was she visible beneath the vine-covered arbor? She'd thought once that he'd paused and looked across the cove and she'd slipped deeper into the shadows beneath the arbor. Now as he neared the cliff's edge, she could scarcely breathe. Who was he? Where had he come from? She felt a stirring deep within, unlike any she'd ever known.

The man took a deep breath, raised his arms, and launched his body. He arched up against the fading blue of the sky, then curved down, down, down.

Camilla leaned forward to watch as he knifed into dark blue water. She imagined the shock of coldness, the plummeting rush downward. How long would it be until he came to the surface?

A faint shout sounded behind her. "Camilla, where are you?

With a rush of gladness, she saw him, his head bulling up out of the water in a froth of bubbles.

The call came again, nearer now. Reluctantly, Camilla turned, moved slowly to the path. She paused for a backward glance. He was stroking toward the rocks, arms slicing cleanly through the water, legs beating a thick white trail of foam. He was a superb swimmer. He would be, of course. No one dives into the sea unless he is a master of the water. He swam toward the rock-buttressed shore where a faint path led up to the bluff. Camilla knew that path well. Many times this past year she'd walked from her villa to this vantage point above the water then restlessly continued on to the path that led down to the rocks. She'd struggled down the steep path to sit in a shallow cave and watch the tide move in and playful porpoises and scuttling crabs.

This was her cove, a quiet and lonely place. Sometimes she brought a picnic basket with cold chicken and bread and cherries for dessert. As she ate in the shade of the arbor, she read poetry or history. The slaves, of course, never questioned her habits, though most Roman matrons wouldn't choose such isolated pleasures.

But she'd never seen the man swimming toward land until these last few weeks.

He reached the rocky shore and rose up out of the water as gracefully as a sea god, his strong limbs only palely visible as the reddening sun began to sink into the west.

"Camilla?" Phoebe's frightened voice carried in the still air.

He was climbing the cliff path, and the rattle of stones masked her call.

Abruptly, Camilla turned and walked quickly down the path toward the villa. She didn't want Phoebe to see him. Phoebe was her slave, loyal to her, loving her, the old nurse she'd brought with her when she married Decimus. Still, she didn't want

Phoebe to see the diver. Camilla wanted to keep to herself those glimpses of grace and beauty.

As she followed the twisting, narrow path, Camilla wondered again where he'd come from, who he was. Not, of course, that his identity could matter to her. She couldn't have eyes for any handsome young men her own age. She knew that. Still, she clung to her remembrance of him. He was extraordinarily handsome. Often, when she was a girl, long before her father arranged her marriage to Decimus, she'd dreamed of love—and of a young man. Her memories of those dreams were pale and indistinct, but the young man had been strong and quick ,with dark curly hair.

"Camilla, where are you?" Phoebe sounded frantic.

"I'm coming," Camilla called out.

They came face to face where the path skirted a cypress.

Phoebe was breathless. "I've been worried. You're late coming in. The sun's almost down. Two letters are waiting for you."

"Letters?"

"I hurried to tell you," Phoebe said quickly, for letters were always an event.

"Who are the letters from?"

"Your husband and your father."

Camilla drew her breath in sharply, began to walk swiftly.

Phoebe hurried after her. "I've brought your cloak."

Camilla shrugged away the cloak. She liked the chill of the evening breeze, the feeling of life in tingling skin. But, as the path angled inland and she strode through the gathering dusk toward the flare of torches that marked the avenue leading up to the villa, her face was as somber as the sea at night, dark and fathomless.

She slowed once to wait for Phoebe. When they reached the base of the hill, the lights from the torches fluttered like ribbons of fire. Camilla paused and stared up the fire-lined avenue. She'd spent her happiest childhood days at the villa. She'd always loved being here, not far from Neapolis. The slender, graceful columns and angled porches sat high on a bluff overlooking the sea.

Decimus loved the villa, too. But not in the same way she did. No, not at all in the same way. He loved its magnificence, the rolling land with vine stocks and gangs of slaves to till the fields. He loved the villa's ornate reception hall and the glorious courtyard with imported trees and shrubs and riots of roses that smelled sweet as Elysium.

Camilla had realized soon after her marriage that Decimus loved all the possessions she brought and would never willingly give up a single one of them. Her villa, but not hers alone since her marriage to Decimus.

She started up the avenue and saw the tall, slender Syrian slave, Priscus, approaching through the dusk. He was spying on her, of course. Camilla knew that. Priscus sent a weekly letter to Decimus, but there wasn't much to report about the mistress except that she took many long walks and worked hard at her studies.

Decimus was proud of her literary knowledge. Camilla moved at ease in the intellectual circles of Rome. She could quote Homer and Virgil, Cicero and Ovid, and so many more. It should have pleased her, perhaps, that Decimus took pride in her accomplishments and, of course, in her beauty. She'd overheard him once, describing her to a friend. "You've not met my wife? Sextus, you'll be thrilled. She's quite lovely with huge violet eyes, like the sea at night, and hair glossy as a raven's wing, and a face that would have rivaled Helen's."

The extravagant praise didn't please her. She was given the credit due any expensive and fine possession, quite like an alabaster vase or a bust of Phrygian marble.

"Yes, Priscus," she said coldly when the slave grew near.

Priscus knew she loathed him. Her disdain seemed to amuse him, which intensified her dislike. He didn't quite smirk, but almost. "A letter from the Master." He held out slate leaves. The two sides closed and sealed to protect the beeswax tablet.

Camilla took the letter without a word. She brushed past him, her sandals crackling against the crushed seashells.

Her father's slave, Demetrius, waited at the villa steps.

Camilla greeted him warmly. "Did your journey go well?"

"Quite well, Miss Camilla."

"My father? How is he?"

Demetrius looked troubled. He'd been with the family for many years, so Camilla listened intently as he leaned close and dropped his voice. "Something is worrying him, something more than the heat and fevers. He's on his way here now."

The heat this summer had parched the vines and curdled the milk of the lambs. An epidemic of fevers was sweeping Rome.

"Is he ill?" Camilla asked anxiously.

The slave shook his head. "No, Miss. But something has upset him. Perhaps he tells you in his letter," and he handed the slate to Camilla.

"Thank you, Demetrius. Go now and rest from your journey." She carried the two letters up broad, shallow steps into the villa, hurrying through the reception hall without a glance at the costly marble busts with their bright gilt and paint or new tapestries hung only this summer. She skirted the shallow basin in the center of the hall and walked through the study to descend the steps into the immense inner courtyard. Her rooms opened beneath the colonnade on the north side. During steamy summer months, the rooms were airless and stuffy, but she wanted to read the letters in privacy.

Several oil lamps gleamed dimly in her room. She sat on the edge of her bed and pulled a small marble-topped table nearer until the flame from a bronze lamp spewed a tiny circle of golden light in her lap.

She took the two tablets, glanced quickly at their seals, dropped Decimus's letter carelessly on the table. She removed the seals and string from her father's letter, opened the leaves of the tablet and began to read the letters scratched in wax.

The letter was brief and puzzling, although it began happily:

> *"Dearest Camilla, I am delighted to inform you that your younger sister, Terentia, will be married next month to Sextus Flavius Pompideus. You know the family, of course."*

Camilla smiled. Certainly she knew the family. It was one of the oldest and wealthiest in Pompeii. She'd been to several weddings there and she wondered which one of the lively boys she'd met had grown to be a man and would now be her sister's husband.

The tablet sagged into Camilla's lap. How odd to think of Terentia as married. Marriage meant . . .

Camilla bit her lip and picked up the tablet. Her eyes skimmed the rest of the message. He described plans under way for the wedding and his hope that she would help with the preparations. As, of course, she would.

It was the last paragraph that made her uneasy.

> *"Camilla, in all confidence, I must also seek your counsel about a very serious matter which affects the family, though I hesitate to burden you with my concern. But you approach life with such a calm and noble demeanor that what you say could have some effect. I will confer with you when I arrive at the villa."*

He closed affectionately, hoping the missive found her well and happy.

The letter sounded so much like her father except for that final disturbing paragraph. The grave cadence of the words brought him perfectly to mind, tall, dignified, stern, a Roman reminiscent of the Republic with its stalwart virtues of courage, steadfastness, and frugality.

His serious approach to life, his emphasis on duty daunted her younger sister, Terentia, and her older sister, Cornelia, but Camilla adored him. Her face softened. She thought him the finest man she'd ever known, the bravest and the noblest. He tried always, in his every act, to pursue the highest ideals, and he expected no less of those around him, especially members of his family.

Perhaps it was fortunate he had no sons. It would be difficult for any man to reach the heights of character exemplified by Senator Publius Cornelius Scipio. Perhaps the disparity between what she admired in her father and what she recognized in her husband accounted in part for her disappointment in her marriage. That and the realization that had slowly come to her about Decimus and his sexual interests.

No one knew how she felt, least of all her father. He was confident he'd made an excellent match for her, just as now he was obviously proud of linking his family to that of the Pompidae with Terentia's marriage.

Camilla knew she was closer to her father than were her sisters, especially since the death of their mother, and he was more likely to ask her counsel than theirs. What kind of problem could affect the family that her father would seek her help?

Camilla frowned in frustration. If only he'd been more specific in his letter. It was maddening to worry and perhaps imagine troubles far greater than might exist. It was unlike her father to send this kind of message, knowing she would be distressed.

Sighing, she snapped shut the tablet. It did no good to borrow trouble. Her father would soon be here and then she'd know. She put the tablet down and slowly picked up the other one, the letter from Decimus.

She had to read what he had written even though she felt cold and distant inside. She broke open the seal without eagerness or interest. She opened the leaves and read quickly, as she might swallow evil tasting medicine. Her shoulders sagged. Decimus would be home within the month.

That was too soon, she thought dully. The governorship of a province always lasted for a year and Decimus had been gone to Sicily for only ten months. Why should he be returning home now?

But the reason for his return didn't matter. What mattered was that he soon would be home and, once again, wherever they stayed, whether in Rome or the Tuscany hills or Lake Larius or here, the night would be filled with the click of dice and loud and drunken shouts as Decimus and his friends gambled, and other sounds, softer sounds, which she didn't want to remember.

Camilla put the tablet down and rose. As she did, her evening girl came through the curtains from her alcove, bringing a basin of fresh water and a clean tunic for sleep. Camilla moved through the nightly ritual with a blank face, but the words thudded in her mind like soldiers marching on the Appian Way: *Decimus is coming home, Decimus is coming home.*

When Camilla lay in her bed, the slave girl blew out the lamps and slipped to her pallet in the alcove. Camilla lay sleepless, watching the soft tracery of moonlight through latticed windows that opened onto the courtyard. It was a balmy night, a night for soft music and quiet voices, but the villa lay silent and somnolent, only the breeze moving in the gardens, rustling the flower-laden bushes and the sweet-scented clinging vines on the arbors, making a sad and gentle and lonely sound like solitary footsteps down a dark street. She drifted slowly into sleep with thoughts of marriage and her father and Decimus's return. Deep into the night, she stirred restlessly and dreamed of a figure high on a cliff, the sun burnishing his body like a flame.

II

"I'm proud of you, Firmus. Everything looks wonderful." Camilla reached up and touched the gleaming leather of a halter, then turned to walk out of the stables.

Firmus hurried after her, beaming with pride. "It will be like old times to have your father here."

Like old times.

Camilla ducked beneath vines sagging from the arbor and welcomed the shade and the chance to hide her face from the overseer.

Like old times. Oh no, never. Not ever again. *Old times* meant summer days when she and Cornelia and Terentia were up at first light for a bowl of porridge then off to their lessons because their father insisted they continue their studies even on vacation. They'd trailed after their Greek teacher as he led them along the beach, quoting passage after passage in purest Attic Greek from the plays of Aristophanes and Menander. *Old times* meant eager hikes, following their father as he spoke to the overseer and slaves. *Old times* meant their mother's soft voice recalling Roman heroes in faraway lands as her daughters helped her weave.

Love permeated the villa then.

Camilla came out the other end of the arbor and blinked in the bright, hot afternoon light. She looked down the neat furrows of the vegetable garden. The leaves of the lettuce, radishes, turnips, and beets glistened with water. A slave girl dipped a watering can and water sprayed ahead of her.

"Firmus, the garden smells good." Camilla breathed deeply of warm earth and dampness and greenery. The rich, summertime scent almost banished the distress evoked by Firmus's reference to old times. Almost.

She left him by the garden, smiling and looking after her with pride and caring. Dear Firmus. At least he was the same.

At the foot of the garden, she turned to look between a double row of plane trees. This was always the first glimpse of the villa on the road from Rome. In the dazzling mid-afternoon sun, the villa glistened, its marble columns and porticoes shining bright as polished ivory. As a child, this gleaming façade spelled the beginning of summer.

This past year, with Decimus gone, she'd spent most of the winter here. She'd welcomed the sweeping winds of winter, walking along the cliff bundled in her cloak, invigorated by the thudding surf.

The villa belonged to her now, part of the dowry given by her father upon her marriage. She should feel an even greater kinship with the land. But she didn't. It was part of her dowry and it bound her to Decimus.

Camilla shook her head wearily, wishing she could shake away her somber thoughts. Her father would be here soon and they would have a wonderful visit. But it was hard to walk between the plane trees and enter the villa, though the shining white house looked just as it had yesterday and last week and last month. But Decimus was coming home and that truth made the reception hall look bleak, despite the vivid colors of the columns and the statues and the soft greens and browns and grays of the pastoral scene painted on the wall to her left. That truth dulled the vivid gold and red threads of the tapestries and bleached the colors from the courtyard.

"Your dinner is ready when you wish," Phoebe announced.

"I'll be a few more minutes," Camilla responded. "I want to check over the financial papers that arrived last week." Camilla's financial agent, a freedman, stayed at the house in Rome, but every month he sent a summary of the latest information on her investments and income from various farms and villas. She wanted to be sure everything was in order to show her father so he would be pleased at her care of her properties.

Camilla carefully checked each report, replaced them in a cupboard in the study. Phoebe stood patiently waiting nearby. Camilla turned and smiled. "Is dinner ready?"

Phoebe nodded. Camilla knew her old nurse hated for her to miss meals so she walked down into the courtyard though she wasn't hungry.

"Paula will play the harp for you," Phoebe said eagerly.

Again, Camilla smiled. Dear Phoebe. She was always disappointed when Camilla ate alone, but Camilla enjoyed the solitude, listening to the soft plucking of the harp and the drone of the bees and occasional harsh screams of the lovely peacocks, that spread their tails and watched as if they knew her thoughts. Tonight she was glad the peacocks couldn't speak and reveal her. Her thoughts swirled as disconsolately as autumn leaves in a November wind.

A young table slave brought warm water and napkins. Camilla washed her hands in a silver bowl, then relaxed as a slave knelt to loosen her sandals and wash her feet. Other slaves moved quietly, their bare feet noiseless against the mosaic pavement, bringing food. Slaves stood on either side of the table and slowly waved huge hand-held fans.

Camilla rested on her left elbow on the eating couch and reached for her silver cup of watered wine. She looked at the table without interest. Eleutheros tried hard to tempt her with special dishes, but she had no appetite for the delicate pastry shell with its succulent filling of shrimp and crab. She picked up a few grapes and carefully chewed around the seeds. She pushed the crust on the pastry dish this way and that, like a child trying to make a dish look eaten. Course followed course. She managed a few tastes from each until, at last, she shook her head at the chief table slave and gestured for her sandals. Again, she washed her hands, and the perfumed water gave off a light scent of lavender.

Camilla slowly walked the length of the courtyard, past the central pool and the fountain where water played from the mouths of dolphins. She loved the courtyard. Usually, the sweet scents and imperious peacocks lifted her spirits, brought peace to her heart, but tonight sadness walked with her.

Camilla stopped at the far end of the courtyard, near a semicircle of rose bushes drooping beneath heavy yellow blooms. A gilded statue of Adonis stood beside a bubbling fountain. Camilla stared at the golden-hued statue glistening in the late afternoon sunlight, the body so perfect. A perfect body.

How long yesterday had she watched the diver poised on the bluff? Not more than a moment or two at most; yet now she could recall him with absolute clarity, his dark curly hair and strong face, the broad span of his chest, the flexed muscles in his legs.

She had attended to many duties today, working hard to be sure the villa would please her father. All day, she'd disciplined her mind, refused to recall that twilight episode, that pointless moment of intimacy, until now as she stood by the golden-limbed statue that idealized the beauty of the male body.

She'd seen a living man more beautiful on those dusky evenings before he dived into the sea. Who was he? Where had he come from? Did he really exist or was he the creation of her own longing, the projection of her desires? Had a man really dived from the cliff last night? Had she seen him those other nights or was she dreaming?

Shrill laughter cut sharply through the stillness of the courtyard.

Camilla stiffened, her face taut and strained. Phoebe knew she didn't want the twins near her. Where were the young boys? Her eyes searched the end of the courtyard. They must be beyond the wall. She glimpsed them as they dashed past the iron gate that opened into the park. They scampered like fawns, two dark boys, twins with tight Grecian curls and brown bodies.

Nausea curled in Camilla's throat. She loathed seeing them, loathed the soft newness of their skin and the bright knowledge in their eyes, loathed what she knew of them and of Decimus.

The boys saw her. They stopped still, both of them, then began to caper and call out in high voices, thin as mountain air, "The master's coming home, the master's coming home."

They didn't mean Camilla's father. The master they served was Decimus.

Camilla steeled her face, but she couldn't control the shudder that rippled deep within her. Abruptly, she strode toward the gate and they began to run, disappearing around the corner of the villa. They knew she never wanted to see them. They knew that she always avoided them if she could. They knew, and she tried to push away the thought, many things and feelings and sensations that Camilla could imagine only in a nightmare.

She didn't look after them. She turned the other direction. Head down, she walked at a furious pace along the shell path, ignoring the beauty of neatly-scythed grass and vine-laden trellises and circular fountains with softly splashing water.

She passed a flock of peacocks, tails spread in iridescent glory. Tame deer, their pelts creamy beige, looked after her curiously. She struck off for the shore path and soon reached the cliff's edge and followed the faint path. She stopped once to catch her breath and stare out at a darkening sea. A sharp breeze penetrated her wool gown, but she welcomed the chill. It helped cool her fiery anger.

She was angry. Violently, sickeningly angry. This anger would one day destroy her. But if she saw the boys and felt no anger, that would be the day she died inside and nothing would ever matter again. Would it be better perhaps to come to that day, to move through life like a husk, empty of yearning but free from pain?

Camilla took a deep breath. The surging water of the cove was just around the next headland. The man she'd watched these past weeks always stood at the highest point to dive. Perhaps he wouldn't be there tonight. Perhaps he'd never been there, was only a beautiful figure in her mind. But she began to walk faster and faster. Only children expect miracles, but she lifted her gown and ran the last few yards. When she came around the curve in the path, she saw the bluff on the other side of the cove. It looked soft and insubstantial in the dusk and it lay as empty as a midnight pavement. Disappointment swept her.

She picked her way carefully up the path, skirting the treacherous edge that crumbled easily, until she reached the highest point of the bluff where he'd stood to dive. Moss and lichens and a few tiny wildflowers clung to life in the crevices of the rock, but human feet left no trace. He might never have stood there. If she hadn't seen him, there would be no way of knowing a man had dived from this cliff.

But she would never forget having seen him.

She stared down at the cove. Dark water surged greedily against the cliff face, the incoming tide pushing the sea higher and higher. The pool was deep now, deep and dark.

Camilla lifted her eyes and stared out at the horizon where the blood-red sun was sinking into the sea. Far off shore, a sailing ship wallowed heavily. One day soon, such a ship would bring Decimus home and then nights at the villa or in Rome would hold the soft laughter of boys and the incessant click of dice.

Just past the headland, she saw a movement in the water. There he was. She'd missed his dive, but he was down below her in the dark water, stroking surely and steadily to shore. In her eagerness, Camilla leaned forward then. At first she felt only unsteadiness. Then, with a sense of horror, the cliff edge crumbled beneath her feet. She plunged into nothingness, flailing to no avail, unable to scream, fear paralyzing her as she plummeted faster and faster, her breath swept away as she tried to call out. Her descent in a way seemed to take forever. She struck the water with brutal force and the water closed over her. She was going down and down. She couldn't breathe as salt water burned her throat, choked her lungs. So this was death, this wild, thrashing agony. Her arms and legs were heavy and consciousness was leaving.

Suddenly strong hands gripped her arms, caught her tight, and she realized dimly that she was being pulled up through the water. The water turned lighter and lighter and then, gasping and choking, she came up out of the water, those strong hands still gripping her.

A strong arm circled her, held her close. "You're safe." The voice was deep and commanding and confident. "I won't let you go."

Still drawing in short desperate breaths, her chest aching, she looked up at his face. Without surprise, she knew her rescuer was the diver from the bluff. He smiled at her and she felt utterly safe.

"My dress is weighting me down," she gasped. "Without your help, I'd never have reached the surface. And now," she twisted to look toward the bluff, "I don't think I can reach shore."

"It's all right. I'm here." He looked toward shore, gauging the strength of the outgoing tide. It would be a hard and furious battle to reach land.

She was breathing better now, though she still felt dizzy and weak. "Let me try to swim. You mustn't endanger yourself."

He looked at her, his dark eyes determined. "I came for you," he said simply. He continued to stare at her. "I've seen you across the cove, little glimpses like the first bird in spring. I wanted to know you." He laughed, sounding carefree and happy. "I had no idea this was how we would meet. But I knew," and his voice was suddenly serious, "that we would meet. I intended to be sure that we met."

Every convention forbade such a statement, but for now, for this moment, she felt free from the restraints of her life, the life she would have lost except for this man. "I came to the cliff to look for you," she blurted out and then was appalled at her honesty.

"For me?"

"I've watched you dive from the cliff." She wanted to say that in the setting sun his body was beautiful. What would he think of her?

He looked at her gravely. "I had thought one evening when you came I wouldn't dive, I would walk around on the path and introduce myself. Tonight I came at my usual time and I knew there was no one beneath the arbor. I waited and finally I dived."

A swell washed over them. He looked again toward shore.

"We'd better go in now." Expertly, he shifted his grip. His arm slipped firmly beneath her breasts and he began to sidestroke toward shore. The water fought them, trying to sweep them out past the headland, out to sea. He paused once and breathed deeply. She felt the heave of his chest.

"Let me swim," she said quickly.

He shook his head. "It's all right. I can save us. Trust me."

Once again he began to stroke toward shore, now just a darker mass against the night sky. Huge swells threw them up and back, but each time he stroked harder until, finally, when she was afraid his lungs would burst, they reached the cliff and wearily pulled themselves up onto a rocky ledge. Breathing heavily, he helped her to her feet, turned her to climb the path ahead of him, and she realized his delicacy in keeping her gaze ahead since he was naked. When they reached the top, she waited, back turned to him, while he pulled on his clothing.

He drew his breath in noisily. Then, gasping, he said, "I told you . . . we could . . . do it."

She turned and reached out to grip his hand. "I owe you my life."

His hand squeezed hers. "Promise me . . ."

"Yes?"

"Promise me . . ." He gulped more air, ". . . you won't go so near the edge again."

"I promise." She added quickly, lightly, "At least, not unless you are near."

He laughed out loud, though a little weakly. Then he looked at her in concern. "You're shivering. Come, I'll take you to my villa. It's just south of here." He paused, said formally, "I'm Marcus Julius Paulus."

She wanted to go with him. She wanted so much to go with him, to be near him for just a little longer. She knew she mustn't.

"So is mine," she said reluctantly. "I'm Camilla Scipio Rufini and I live at Swallow's Nest."

He would know the villa, of course. Her villa was famous along the coast for its graceful beauty.

"Swallow's Nest," he repeated slowly. He reached out and took her other hand, long enough to touch her wedding ring, then he let her hands drop.

Camilla shivered again.

"I'll take you to your home," he said quietly. Without another word, he reached out and lifted her into his arms, carrying her as easily as he would a child. For just an instant, Camilla stiffened, then, slowly, she relaxed and rested her head against his shoulder. She could walk. She knew she should tell him to put her down, that she was strong enough to manage.

She didn't say a word.

III

"Such an escape you had, Ma'am." Galla tugged gently on Camilla's thick black hair. "Your beautiful hair is all matted and wild this morning." The slave girl worked and pulled until the comb's ivory teeth slipped through the tangle. "Weren't you scared to death?"

Camilla sat on a backless chair while her hairdresser worked. Galla had chattered non-stop ever since she'd come to Camilla's room soon after breakfast. The story must have burst like a geyser among the slaves, so Decimus would have a full report from Priscus. It would be interesting to know what Decimus would think of her near-drowning. She'd never had any inkling what Decimus truly thought about anything, except gambling and the little slave boys. Even there she could only conjecture because, of course, they never spoke of those things. They talked of crops and weather and dinners and friends, much like strangers meeting for the first time at a banquet.

"The Master will be glad you were saved, Ma'am."

Camilla moved restlessly.

"Oh there, did I hurt you? I'm sorry, I didn't mean to tug too hard."

"That's all right, Galla."

"The gentleman who saved you, Ma'am, isn't it a lucky thing he'd come here to live."

To live. Camilla's face didn't change, but she felt a wild surge of excitement. Slaves would know all about new arrivals in the neighborhood. The slaves loved to gossip.

"I scarcely learned more than his name," Camilla said carefully.

"Of course you didn't," said Galla sympathetically. "You were like a drowned rat, Ma'am, if you'll forgive me for saying so. They say he carried you up the avenue and you were all of a heap, wet through and chilled to the bone. Phoebe screamed and called for help and they rushed you to your room and lighted a brazier and wrapped you in warm, dry wool, and Phoebe rubbed and massaged to get the life back in your limbs. They do say you were pale as death itself."

"I should have thanked him," Camilla prodded.

"Everybody thanked him, and Firmus told him that whatever the villa has was his to share for now and always and for his family, too."

"His family?" Camilla asked sharply.

"Don't you know, Ma'am? He came to the coast about a month ago to take over the villa. His father, Senator Paulus, bought it two years ago and this Marcus is his oldest son and the apple of his eye. He's going to be a great advocate like Cicero. He's just finished his studies in Athens and he's come here to work on some cases he's going to present in Rome next month. They'll be his first."

Camilla remembered the strength in his arms and the warmth of his body and the bright and lively intelligence in his dark eyes. His voice was deep and strong, just as a great orator's should be.

"So he moved here a month ago," Camilla said slowly. "His

must be the villa south of ours, the small one with the red marble columns."

"That's the one." Galla leaned to her left, intent on teasing Camilla's thick dark hair into a soft mound of curls. Usually Camilla was too impatient to sit for long, but this morning she sat quite still while Galla fussed and teased her brilliant dark tresses into a shimmering cascade of ringlets.

"You said something about Marcus's family. Is . . . is his wife here with him?"

Galla didn't answer for a moment, absorbed in arranging a curl just so. Then she said sympathetically, "Oh, no, Ma'am, it's too bad. He isn't married. It would be so nice for you to have someone your own age so near."

Camilla looked into her hand mirror, a shining oval plate of highly polished silver. Her image glimmered softly. Slowly, she smiled. The brightness of the silver couldn't match the brightness in her heart.

"There, Ma'am, that's just perfect if I do say so myself."

For the first time in so long, Camilla really studied her reflection. Her vividly black hair curled softly, the kind of curls a man would love to touch.

"Thank you, Galla. My hair looks very nice."

The hairdresser looked pleased. She smiled and began to gather up her combs and brushes.

"Tell Anna to bring my lilac gown."

"I'll tell her, Ma'am."

Camilla tried on three gowns before she was satisfied, settling finally for a soft wool in a delicate shade of peach. She spent half an hour selecting her jewelry, choosing a gold filigree necklace and gold earrings that jangled lightly as she walked.

Outside her bedroom, Camilla paused under the colonnade in the cool sweep of shade to look at the courtyard. The midmorning sun blazed. The three fountains splashed cheerfully. Camilla smiled. How wonderful to be alive this glorious day, this magnificent, brilliant, beautiful day.

Phoebe joined her. "Camilla, you look wonderful this morning. There's a magic about you. I've never seen you look lovelier." But she looked puzzled as well as pleased. A new slave might guess that her mistress' flush of beauty came in response to the news that her husband was coming home. Phoebe wasn't a new slave.

"It's a lovely day," Camilla said lightly. "I believe I'll read in the library."

Phoebe followed her. "That's sensible. A nice, restful way to spend the day. It will help you regain your strength after your awful fright last night. Oh dear, your father will blame me that I wasn't with you when it happened."

"It wasn't your fault, Phoebe. Papa knows I like to walk alone. Next time, I won't go so near the edge."

"Oh Camilla, you won't go back there, will you?"

"Of course I'll go back."

Phoebe followed her into the library, clucking unhappily. Camilla stopped by one of the tall wooden racks that held scrolls in circular cubbyholes. Scrolls with red tassels were histories. Gold tassels marked plays, orange tassels poetry, and brown tassels agricultural works. Camilla picked out a scroll with an orange tassel. She stretched out comfortably on a couch near the entrance to the courtyard. A gentle breeze wafted over her.

Phoebe hovered at the end of the couch. "Will you tell your father I always asked to go with you?"

"Phoebe, stop worrying. Papa isn't going to blame you. Besides, you couldn't have done a thing to help even if you'd been there."

"I could have run for help."

"There wouldn't have been time. Our new neighbor was swimming past the headland when he saw me fall. And he almost didn't reach me in time."

"Oh, Miss Camilla!"

"But he did, so don't fret."

"Your father will want to meet him."

Camilla nodded. "I'll have a dinner for Papa and we'll invite several neighbors, including Marcus."

"That's very thoughtful, Camilla."

After Phoebe left, Camilla unrolled the scroll, but she didn't read. Instead, she said his name over and over again to herself, *Marcus Julius Paulus, Marcus Julius Paulus, Marcus Julius Paulus.*

The scroll slipped to her lap.

He would come today. She felt a deep certainty. She wanted him to come. She was going to see him again, his brilliant dark eyes, his bold nose and full mouth.

Happiness ebbed. What good would it do to see him? She was a married woman and her husband was even now traveling home. That, of course, would be no hindrance to many of her friends. In reality, the fact of a husband, present or absent, posed no boundaries to most of her friends. Livia dallied with her husband's best friend. Paula slipped away in the quiet of the afternoon siestas to meet a young student. And there was Julia. How many lovers had Julia known? Five? Seven? More?

But she wasn't Livia or Paula or Julia. She was Camilla Scipio Rufini and her father, Senator Publius Cornelius Scipio, symbolized the best that Rome stood for. Her father believed in her.

Camilla reached out for her bell. She wouldn't ask Marcus to dinner. No. She'd write him a formal thank you and ask her father to go and meet him. But, she, Camilla, would stay aloof because—

"Mistress." The little slave girl slipped into the library, her eyes dancing with excitement. "You have a caller. In the reception hall. The man who carried you home last night."

Camilla's heart thudded. She came to her feet, torn between eagerness and uncertainty. She lifted her head and turned to walk into the reception hall.

He waited by the square pool, his hands clasped behind his back.

Camilla knew how she should handle this interview. She would be gracious yet formal, appreciative yet distant.

He turned to face her.

He was even larger than she remembered, powerfully built, thick-chested and broad-shouldered. For the first time, she saw his face in full light, deep-set intelligent eyes, a bold nose, a blunt chin.

They stared at each other in a moment of silence as intense as a shout.

He took a step toward her. "You look wonderful."

She thrilled to the sound of his deep voice.

He walked slowly toward her and stood so near she could have reached out and touched him. She wanted terribly to touch him and to feel again the warmth and strength of his hands.

"I can never thank you enough," she said stiffly.

His face was grave. "Seeing you is the only thanks I need."

Camilla wondered if he felt the same sweep of emotion she was experiencing. She knew she must step away, put some distance between, or she was going to do something wonderfully forbidden.

She stepped back a pace. She should thank him again, make some comment about matters requiring her attention, bid him goodbye. Instead, her voice a little breathless, she asked, "Would you like to come and walk in the park? Our flowers are very famous."

"I'd like that very much."

They went together down the broad steps into the courtyard and followed the central path to the far end. He opened the gate. The park spread before them, empty except for a flock of peacocks. They walked up an oyster-shell path. Water from an early morning sprinkling clung to the leaves of apple trees and lay in little pools at the base of the rose bushes.

"Your villa is certainly well cared for. Mine needs quite a bit of work."

Camilla looked at the formally trimmed lawn. "My overseer has worked especially hard these last few days. My father is coming on a visit and Firmus wants him to be pleased with the property." She paused, added, "The villa was part of my dowry."

The texture of the air between them changed, as if a thin cloud obscured the sun, chilling the ground. They walked a few more steps and stopped beside an oblong pool with red and gold tiles around its rims and a marble dolphin spewing water at its center.

Marcus looked down at her. "Does your husband take a great interest in the villa?"

Camilla looked back at the villa, graceful and lovely in the brilliant sunlight. Then she faced Marcus. "Yes," she said drily. "He takes a keen interest." She paused, added coolly, deliberately, "The villa is quite profitable."

The distance between them seemed to increase. "You must take great pride in it," Marcus said formally.

"Do I?" she asked lightly. "Not really, but I don't want my father to be disappointed."

Marcus stared at her, puzzled, unable to reconcile her

mercenary appraisal with her disclaimer of interest. He asked, almost reverentially, "Is your father Senator Scipio?"

"Yes."

"He was once one of Rome's greatest orators."

Camilla smiled. "I know. At least, I've been told that he was. Mother told me about some of his best trials."

Marcus leaned forward. "Perhaps I shouldn't ask, but I've always wondered. Why did he stop taking cases?"

Camilla shook her head. "I don't know, Marcus. I can only guess because he's never said. My mother told me once it was because of the kind of man he is. He stands for the kind of values we treasured under the Republic: rectitude, honesty, devotion to duty. She said that he didn't believe that Romans measured up to the heroes of the past and he wasn't going to spend his life championing men who didn't deserve to wear the toga."

"He must be tough as an eagle."

"He is," Camilla said proudly, "he is. I want you to meet him. Will you come for dinner when he arrives?" So much for her resolve to send this man away.

"I'd like to come. I'd very much like to come." His dark eyes smiled at her. "I'd like to meet your father, whether or not he was Senator Scipio."

"What a nice thing to say."

Camilla saw the desire in his eyes and feelings stirred that she'd never known before. She wanted to touch him and be touched in ways that she'd never known, only dreamed of. Abruptly, she turned away and walked up the path. How could she think thoughts such as these? And how could she think such thoughts on the heels of speaking of her father, who loved her so much and admired her as the kind of Roman matron a woman should be. If he knew she had thoughts such as these, he would be dismayed. More, he would be heartbroken.

Marcus hurried to catch up. Just ahead willow trees bent near a lake. A marble bench sat deep within the willows, in a lacy, shadowy hideaway. Camilla brushed aside drooping fronds and sank down on the bench. She stared out at the blue water, brazenly bright beneath the midday sun.

Marcus followed her into the shaded retreat.

She looked up with a bright and social smile. "I understand you've just returned from several years of study in Greece?'

He stood over her and she was conscious of his height and strength. He could easily pick her up. Last night, he'd carried her in his arms. To be held in his arms . . .

He gazed at her soberly, recognizing the distance she'd set. "Yes," he said agreeably. "Yes, I did." He smiled, a slow smile that she was beginning to recognize. "May I sit with you?"

She didn't speak, but, at her slow nod, he pushed aside the fronds and took his place beside her. It was a small bench. She felt his arm touching hers. She stared determinedly out at the brassy blue water.

"Have you been to Athens?" he asked.

"Yes. Several years ago, Papa took us on a tour."

They talked of their favorite views. They found that they liked the same places, the same plays, the same famous statues and paintings.

"Have you ever written a play?" she asked eagerly.

He laughed. "I have a glib tongue, but playwriting's too much for me." He studied her. "You've written plays, haven't you?"

She clapped her hands together. "How did you know?"

He stared into her eyes. "The way you spoke of drama revealed more than the interest of a playgoer. I know we've only spent minutes together, but I feel like I know much about you. You admire your father and that tells me that you respect goodness and honor. The villa is beautifully kept up which means you are in tune with the seasons and that you have an eye for beauty. Last night when I carried you to the door, the shock of your near loss brought tears and then joy that you were saved, which means you are a beloved mistress. And yet, there is so much more I want to know about you." His glance held hers with burning intensity.

He must leave, Camilla thought wildly. She mustn't stay here with the touch of his body against her.

"Camilla," he said softly. His arm slipped around her.

"Marcus . . . Marcus, we mustn't . . ."

Gently, so gently, he bent down and his lips touched hers, delicately as a rosebud unfolds.

Camilla reached up to touch his cheek. She knew she should pull away, but she wanted to stay in his embrace forever. Her hand slipped to the back of his neck and it felt smooth and warm, and then her fingers touched his wiry, black hair.

They parted for an instant.

Hesitatingly, her lips brushed his cheek, and sought his mouth. As they kissed again, gently, Camilla felt a tumultuous sweep of warmth, a sensation she'd never known before. Abruptly, she pulled free. "I'm sorry," she said, her face flaming. "I can't imagine what you think of me."

Of course, it was obvious what he must think. He must believe she was like many Roman matrons, available now or tomorrow for any man's hand. The flush on her cheeks deepened. She struggled to her feet and began to run down the path.

"Camilla," his deep voice called.

This time she didn't stop.

IV

Priscus stood by the gate to the courtyard, his bright blue tunic a blaze of color next to pink wall. He was waiting for her.

The knowledge of his surveillance deepened the red of her cheeks. She would have brushed past him without a word, but he called out. “Mistress, are you all right?”

Camilla paused and looked at him inquiringly.

He returned her gaze boldly, his pale gray eyes sharp and curious.

She hated his appearance, his balding head and pale skin and bulging cheeks like those of an overfull water rat. “Why shouldn’t I be all right?” Her stare was cold.

His eyes slithered away. “You were walking so fast.”

“I like to walk fast.”

“But I thought you were in the garden with the young man who saved you from the sea,” he said slyly.

“Did you?” she retorted. “He has gone home.”

“Oh no, ma’am. Here he comes up the path.”

Camilla turned to face Marcus, well aware of Priscus’s greedy, interested eyes.

Marcus strode up to them.

He would be discreet, of course. Camilla’s cheeks reddened

again. How far had she lost control of herself that she should need for a man to be discreet in the presence of her husband's slave? The thought stiffened her so she was able to say quite easily, "Hello there. I thought you'd gone home."

He answered as smoothly. "I was on my way and realized I'd neglected to thank you for the dinner invitation. Do you expect your father tonight?"

Camilla nodded. "Yes. I'll look forward to seeing you."

"It will be my pleasure. It isn't often that a new advocate has the opportunity to meet such a famous orator."

Camilla smiled. It was the perfect comment for Marcus to make. Priscus would fit that remark into his knowledge of the neighbor and it would all seem very natural. But Priscus couldn't see Marcus' eyes. They said other things and she knew it wasn't oratory that excited him. She must talk to him, make it clear she wasn't available.

Camilla said briskly, "I'll see you at dinner," and turned away. As she walked up the path, she thought how strange that moment was. Two men watched her, one a slave and her enemy, the other a man who would love her if she let him, and neither knew her thoughts.

As she entered the courtyard, a house slave ran to her. "Mistress, your father is here."

Camilla lifted her skirt and ran. He stood waiting in the reception hall. He held up his arms and she ran into his embrace and clung to him. "Papa, it's been so long since I've seen you."

"Camilla, dearest." His voice was gruff and tired. He gave her a hard hug, held her a little away to look down into her face. "What's this I hear about you falling from the cliff?"

She tried to make light of it, but Phoebe stood nearby and she broke into a high excited recital of the cliff crumbling beneath Camilla's feet and her near escape from drowning.

Camilla's father frowned darkly. "You were on the cliff path alone at dusk?"

Camilla slipped an arm through her father's and turned him toward the steps. "Let's go out to the courtyard and I'll have some wine brought to you. Papa, of course, I was out by myself. I'm a grown woman and I can walk about my land in the evening if I wish. I do so almost every night." When her father's frown deepened, she said lightly, "Don't worry, Papa. I won't go near the edge next time."

"Camilla, it could have been—"

"But it wasn't," she interrupted. "And you'll have a chance to meet our new neighbor tonight and thank him."

"That I will do."

The tone of her father's voice brought the quick prick of tears to her eyes. How wonderful to know she was loved. If she ever doubted that her father cared, his voice as he said those four words reassured her for always.

In the bustle of calling for water and wine and for an awning to be rigged near the central fountain, Camilla had a chance to study her father. What she saw dismayed her. He'd always been tall above the average with crisply black hair and a tanned, strong face. Now there were silver threads in his hair. His face looked ravaged and worn. Deep lines bracketed his mouth. His shoulders were bowed, as if he carried a heavy weight.

"Papa, have you been ill?" she asked worriedly.

"No." But his voice was heavy, somber. He didn't meet her gaze. Instead, he sat down on a marble bench, his back straight, as always, but he stared emptily into the rushing waters of the fountain.

She could see him in profile, his bony beak of a nose, his taut, thin mouth, but, for the first time in his life, there was an aura of defeat about him. Something must be terribly wrong. Camilla remembered the final, disturbing paragraph in his letter. Before she could frame a question, and she hesitated to break his grim silence, he looked up at her, visibly forced a smile, and asked, "Will you help me plan Terentia's wedding?"

"Of course, Papa. I'd love to help. Have you chosen the date?"

He nodded. "The priest made a sacrifice last week and studied the entrails. We've chosen the Ides of September."

Camilla smiled. So her little sister would take a husband next month. September would be a beautiful month for a wedding, especially if the newlyweds took a wedding trip to the sea.

For just an instant, Camilla pictured in her mind a rugged coastline and a darkening pool of water and a man poised to dive.

"I'll do everything I can," Camilla said hastily, pushing away that image. At this moment, of all times, how could she think of him? "I want everything to be perfect for Terentia."

Camilla's father smiled fondly at her. "My dear Camilla, you are always a comfort to me. With a daughter such as you, I've never regretted the lack of a son. And, of course, your husband has been a source of pride to all of us."

Camilla's face smoothed into an expression of emptiness, as devoid of feeling as a marble statue's. "Tell me," she said quickly, "what do you think of Terentia's husband to be?"

"Sextus is a fine fellow. His family is superior. They've run Pompeii for years."

"Is Terentia happy?"

Her father nodded slowly, "I think so. Of course, it's hard for a man to know." He frowned. "I wish your mother could be here. I miss your mother. She and I . . . we admired each other."

The words were formal, but behind them lay years of caring and thoughtfulness. Camilla remembered clearly her mother's light bell-like laughter and her gentle teasing ways with her husband and her refusal to let him be dour or gruff.

"She could have been such a help to me in choosing husbands for our daughters," the senator continued. He reached out to pat Camilla's shoulder. "At least I did the right thing for you, Camilla."

Water splashed merrily in the fountain. A peacock in the far corner of the patio spread his magnificent tail, gave his raucous cry.

Camilla looked away from her father. If ever she would tell him the truth, this was the moment. If he knew, surely he would let her come home, despite his horror of divorce. Of course, he would oppose her ever marrying again. Once again, unbidden, she remembered the magnificent body of a man poised to dive. She took a deep breath, half turned to speak, and was stricken to silence by the pain in her father's face.

The senator stared into the fountain but he was seeing something that wounded him deeply.

"Papa, what's wrong?"

He looked at her searchingly. "You've spent most of this past year here at the villa, haven't you?"

The question surprised her. "Yes. Most of it. I went back to Rome for the Saturnalia." She'd almost stayed at the villa for the holiday, but so many friends invited her to parties during the big December festival and it was fun to be in Rome for the races and the topsy-turvy time when the slaves were waited on by their families. Camilla had bought Phoebe a beautiful linen robe from Egypt. And, of course, it was fun to exchange gifts with friends and family. Her father had been absent on a journey to Britain for the Emperor.

She smiled at her father. "I missed seeing you. Did you find the presents I left for you?"

Her father managed a smile in return. "You're always so thoughtful, Camilla. You know how interesting I find Seneca's ideas and I especially appreciated receiving his newest work."

The thought of Saturnalia and her father's presence combined to bring back other memories. "Papa, do you remember when we were little and you always warned us there wouldn't be any gifts if we were naughty . . ." Her voice trailed away because, once again, he looked so anguished.

"Camilla, have you talked to any of your friends from Rome lately?"

It was an innocuous question, but the tone of his voice filled her with dread. "There's always someone passing through this time of year," she responded uncertainly. "Julia Calvus was here last week on her way to her villa. We had a good visit. A few days before that, Livia and Julius Marius stayed overnight."

Her father's face hardened. "Julia Calvus. Isn't she the one who's been married five times?"

Was it five times or six? Camilla had lost count. But she'd known Julia since they were schoolgirls. "Julia's been married several times," Camilla said mildly.

"It's disgusting," her father said harshly, striking his fist against his leg. "She doesn't deserve to be a Roman."

Camilla thought of Julia's visit. Julia drank too much, diluted by too little water. She'd even cast interested looks at the slave who'd taken off her sandals at dinner. She looked years older than her age.

"Papa, I feel sorry for Julia."

"Sorry for her? Why, she's nothing better than a whore." Then, quickly, he said, "I'm sorry, Camilla, to use such a word in front of you. I apologize."

Camilla shook her head gently. Poor Papa. He couldn't imagine some of the words she'd heard at parties these last few years. At a few of the parties they'd attended, at Decimus's insistence, there'd been happenings her father would never have dreamed possible. It sickened Camilla to recall one particular banquet at Julia's. The men used feathers to tickle their throats so they would vomit and then eat more. The drinking that night had been wild and uncontrolled. Two young men who'd been at the banquet were found drowned in the Tiber the next morning. Ugly rumors swirled through Roman society: It was a suicide pact; No, it was murder, one of them had insulted Caligula the week before; No, it was an accident, they'd both drunk too much, then tried to swim across the river on a dare.

Later, Camilla told Decimus she never wanted to go to another party at that house. Decimus only laughed. "You're too sensitive," he'd said. "We can't take the woes of the world on our shoulders. Besides, I had a very good time that night. I won 30,000 sesterces."

"It's all right, Papa," Camilla said gently. "But please . . ." She paused. She wanted to urge her father not to be so harsh in his judgment of Julia. But Julia's behavior was anathema to everything he held dear. She tried to think of words that wouldn't anger him. "Papa, do you remember when we were little girls, Julia and I?"

He nodded grimly.

"Julia always had a favorite doll," Camilla recalled. "A little old rag of a doll that she'd had forever. She carried it everywhere and pretended it was a baby. She loved it so much. She told me, the way girls tell each other, how much she wanted someday to have babies and to love them."

"That's what Roman girls should dream of. It's a disgrace that she's gone so far from the ways she was taught."

"She tried," Camilla said quietly. "She had a beautiful baby just a year after she and Gnaeus were married. Someone who saw the baby told me she was so pretty, tiny with bright dark eyes and just a little wisp of dark hair."

Senator Scipio frowned. "I didn't know Julia had any

children." He shook his head, "It'd be a disgrace to a child to have a mother whose name is known to every man in Rome."

Camilla smoothed her dress. "No, Julia isn't a mother now. Gnaeus decided he didn't want a daughter for a first child so he had the baby taken and left on the dump."

For a long moment, the only sound was of water splashing in the fountain.

"I've always opposed exposing children," he said finally.

But any Roman father had that choice, to accept a baby or not, to bring it up or expose it at the dump. Often, of course, slave traders took abandoned babies for future investment. Sometimes, too, childless families would seek out these children.

So Julia's baby might still live.

But Camilla imagined Julia's agony. To bear a child, to hold and suckle her for a few days, then to picture that tiny bundle crying amid the refuse, crying and crying until her infant's voice was gone and there was only a hoarse, desperate mew and then, finally, nothing. That was frightful but to hope for life and know that more often than not children taken from the dump heap ended up in dark cubicles for the use and pleasure of adults with twisted and strange desires. That would be worse.

"I didn't know," her father said quietly. He sighed. "But a Roman matron should hold herself higher than Julia has chosen."

Camilla didn't answer. Surely her father understood that heartbreak could ruin a woman. Not everyone had his strength, and, a tiny disloyal thought darted, he'd never had to face a personal crisis of that kind. His wife had been a woman everyone admired. And she had loved him.

Love, Camilla thought sadly, didn't come to everyone.

"Every family should have children," her father continued. "Children seal the family, make it strong." He shook his head.

"Not enough children are being born. I don't know what's wrong with Romans today."

Camilla made no answer here, either. She hugged her arms to her body despite the searing afternoon heat. If her father was inquiring, ever so delicately, about her lack of children, she had nothing to say. Nothing at all. At least she'd never have to bear Decimus a child. Funny, Julia's heart broke because she bore a child. Camilla felt only relief that children would never be hers. More to distract her father than for any other reason, she asked, "Have you seen Julius and Fabius lately?" They were the four and six-year-old sons of her older sister, Cornelia, her father's adored grandsons.

His face brightened. "They spent a week with me recently. You won't believe how big Sextus has grown. He's going to be a big man."

Camilla smiled. "Cornelia, how is she?"

Once again the mask of misery covered his face. "Camilla, I asked about your friends from Rome because I didn't know if you had heard. There are dreadful stories going around about Cornelia."

"About Cornelia?" Her lively and bright and fun sister. Her beloved sister.

The senator nodded heavily.

Now Camilla understood her father's distress. Cornelia was his eldest daughter, tall and slim and regal, with shining coppery hair and brilliant green eyes, a strikingly beautiful woman. His eldest daughter and his pride.

"Have you heard anything of it?" he asked again. His eyes watched her anxiously and she saw the tiny quiver of hope that perhaps what he had been told wasn't so.

"I haven't seen much of Cornelia lately," Camilla responded, but she looked away from her father's searching eyes. "I've been down here at the villa and I was only in Rome over the Saturnalia. I saw her then and she looked wonderful, as always."

Wonderful, but different.

Camilla wasn't going to say that. She wasn't going to describe the high spots of color in her sister's face, her frantic, rapid talk, her laughter that shrilled higher and higher as the banquet progressed. Camilla leaned forward and dipped her hand into the fountain and welcomed the coolness of the water. Her long, soft hair fell forward, too, hiding her face from her father's imploring eyes.

"Cornelia and Titus are quite social," Camilla continued. "They are at the palace a lot. Decimus and I have not spent much time there." From what Camilla had heard of the banquets, she was grateful that she and Decimus weren't invited there often.

Her father nodded. "Titus is one of the Emperor's favorites. I've always thought that was wonderful for Cornelia, but now I am not sure."

He didn't have to explain. Camilla knew about the wild parties at the palace and about Caligula's rumored fondness for his sisters and other women, too, and his erratic, often cruel, behavior.

"You haven't heard any rumors about Cornelia?" her father pressed.

Camilla shook her head. "What kind of stories are going about?"

Her father avoided her eyes. "I don't know exactly."

"Tell me, Papa."

"I was at the Baths," he said harshly. "Having a massage. Some men came in and took their places on the next tables. They were talking about a banquet they'd been to the night before. One of them asked, 'Who's the woman who was with the gladiator?

The tall, redheaded woman?' The second one said. He said, 'Oh, that's Titus Maro's wife. They say she'll only bed the gladiator who's won that day.'"

Cornelia Scipio Maro. Titus' wife. Camilla's elder sister. Senator Scipio's daughter.

Tall and redheaded. The description fit Cornelia, but Camilla said quickly, "Papa, you may have misunderstood the name."

Wearily, he shook his head.

"People say things sometimes because they want to believe them," Camilla continued. "You know how lovely Cornelia is. A lot of men would like to believe she's that kind of woman."

"I made no mistake." He looked at her imploringly. "Camilla, will you talk to Cornelia?"

Now Camilla knew why her father had come from Rome. But what did he expect her to do? Was she supposed to ask, "My sister, are you truly sleeping with gladiators?" How would Cornelia respond? What right had Camilla to ask that kind of question of anyone, much less the sister she adored? "Papa, I don't think I should."

"Then you think it's true." He sprang up from the bench and walked away from her.

Camilla hurried after him. "Wait, Papa, I didn't mean that. I just didn't think it would be right to ask her that kind of question."

"But if it's true?" he asked brokenly. He gazed at her with tears in his eyes. "I must know the truth."

Camilla reached out, touched his arm. "Papa, don't be upset. I'll talk to Cornelia."

Her father looked relieved and hopeful. "I knew you'd help me. You can talk to Cornelia. Make her see that she needs to be more . . . thoughtful in her public actions. Sometimes matters can appear to be very unsavory and, really, there's nothing to it." He slipped his arm around Camilla's shoulders. "You're a fine woman, Camilla, just like your mother. You're the kind of Roman matron the world respects. Cornelia will listen to you."

V

Camilla stood in the open archway that led from the study into the courtyard. She shaded her eyes against the mid-afternoon sun. Everything looked lovely. The water in the three fountains arched high, glittering brightly. A peacock paced slowly past, his magnificent tail feather glistening. Her father would be pleased. Awnings hung over the couches that sat on three sides of the marble dining table. It was always more pleasant to eat outdoors in the summer.

Camilla hurried down the steps. She plumped up the cushions on the couches. It would be especially comfortable to dine tonight because each couch would hold only two diners instead of three. She and her father would share the host couch. Claudia and Publius Albus would sit to their left and an old friend of her father's, Tiberius Capito, would share a couch with Marcus.

What would it be like to be near Marcus again? A faint flush stained her cheeks. He must think of her as men apparently thought of her sister. How dreadful it would be if her father ever learned that she had been in Marcus's arms for that brief and tentative kiss that burned so brightly in her memory.

Camilla walked briskly to the colonnade. Her father must

never know. And she and Marcus must not be alone together again.

"My lady."

Camilla started. Damn Priscus. He crept about as quietly as a water snake. When Decimus returned, she was going to insist that Priscus be sent to another of their houses. She wasn't going to tolerate his presence, always underfoot. After all, this villa belonged to her, not to Decimus. But none of this showed in her face. She turned slowly and gave him a bored glance. "Yes, Priscus."

"Tiberius Capito has arrived, my lady."

Camilla nodded and turned to go to the reception hall. Her father came down the colonnade. "Is old Tiberius here already?"

Camilla nodded. "You know he's always prompt, Papa."

They walked together through the courtyard and up the steps. When they reached the reception hall, the two men embraced, then Tiberius turned to Camilla. "My dear, you get prettier every year. But I understand that young man of yours is off on duty?"

It took a moment for Camilla to equate the description with Decimus. After a tiny pause, she nodded. "Decimus is serving as governor of Syria, but he'll be home soon."

"Things will be gayer here when the master's back," Tiberius said.

The three of them walked together toward the courtyard, Tiberius booming cheerfully and her father responding in kind. Suddenly, the whole evening seemed intolerable to Camilla. Her life was a performance. She lived behind a mask just as much as any actor at the theater. Her young man. How hurtful that was.

The Albuses arrived. Claudia swooped down on Camilla. "My dear, what's this I hear about you almost drowning the other day? Here you are my nearest neighbor and I didn't even find out until this afternoon. Why, at first I didn't believe a word of it. I said, Camilla wouldn't fall off a cliff. She's as surefooted as a goat. Of course, you're much prettier than a goat but I could scarcely believe what I heard."

At the top of the steps, Priscus announced, "Marcus Julius Paulus."

Camilla forced herself to turn slowly, but her heart pounded. He stood on the steps in his white toga. The breeze rustled the cloth against him and moved in his thick curly dark hair.

Camilla's father reached him first. "You're the man who saved my daughter's life." The senator embraced Marcus. "Whenever I can be of service to you, I will be."

Marcus looked toward Camilla, his dark eyes intense. "I'm happy I was there. I want . . ."

Camilla drew her breath in sharply.

". . . your daughter to be well and happy."

Camilla moved toward them, smiling lightly. "I'm very well and happy tonight. With good friends and family about me, how can I be otherwise?"

Everyone took his place on the couches. They reclined on their left elbows against the soft and richly decorated pillows. As the slaves washed the guests' hands and removed their sandals to wash their feet, Marcus's gaze held hers until she wrenched her eyes away. She must steel herself, look at others. A lingering glance would reinforce Marcus's judgment of her as a temptress. Determinedly, Camilla looked at her father.

Her father smiled at her, then turned toward his old friend, "Do you remember that time, Tiberius, when we had the Gauls on the run?"

The older men entertained with anecdotes of their service years while Claudia chattered non-stop to Camilla about the latest hairstyle fashions and how she'd bought a new Greek slave to do her hair because, after all, you had to have an expert and the new style was just too much for her Syrian girl.

Every so often, Camilla would look up to see Marcus watching her.

She wished Marcus would be more careful. If her father noticed, he would be disturbed. But her father was deep in conversation with Tiberius, so, just for an instant, Camilla looked fully at Marcus, and she felt as she had when his lips touched hers. Abruptly, she turned her face away. She knew her cheeks were flaming and Claudia was looking at her in surprise. Quickly, Camilla plunged into a description of plans for Terentia's wedding and there was general conversation as the last of the courses came.

They finished with a dessert of cake. The Albuses were the first to leave as shadows fell. When the slaves cleared away the dishes, Tiberius turned to her father, "Would you like to see that new mare of mine, Publius? She's a beauty."

Senator Scipio turned to his daughter. "I believe I'll walk over to Tiberius' stable for a while, Camilla."

Camilla smiled and her heart had an odd, uneven, up-and-down sensation. "Of course, Papa."

Camilla didn't look toward Marcus as they washed their hands and regained their sandals. Her father said, "Perhaps Marcus will walk with you this evening, Camilla, and I won't have to worry about your safety."

"I'd like that very much," Marcus replied.

Camilla knew she should decline. She could say she was tired. She could smile and send Marcus on his way. Instead, without a word, she let Marcus take her elbow and they began to walk toward the gate that led into the park.

She did stop at the gate and half turn toward him. "Marcus, this afternoon, I didn't mean . . ."

"Let's go this way, Camilla."

They passed through the gate. Once again, Camilla stopped. This time so quickly that Marcus asked, "What's wrong?"

Part of her mind wondered in surprise at his quick perception. The other part struggled with the anger boiling inside her. She stared down the pathway. Marcus frowned and looked, too, then called out sharply, "Who goes there? Come this way."

The twins ran lightly toward them, looking like fawns startled by a hunter. They giggled as they skittered by Camilla. They slanted to their right, running back toward the villa.

Camilla stared after them, her body rigid.

"Tell me what's wrong," Marcus urged. "Who are they?"

"I can't bear to see them."

"Camilla, why not?"

She looked up at him, her face twisted. "That shocks you, doesn't it? You must wonder why I said that of young boys, how I can speak with such anger. You must think me not only a wanton but a horrible creature." Abruptly, she ducked her head and turned away from him and began to run across the neatly-scythed grasses toward the path that led to the cliffs.

He caught up with her easily. She'd known that he would and yet she'd had to run. She couldn't tell him. She'd already given more of herself than she'd ever dreamed she could to a stranger. He was, of course, a stranger, no matter how she felt when she was near him.

He reached out and took her hand in his warm grasp and walked with her, swiftly. They walked together, their strides long and matching. As the cool evening breeze off the sea whipped against them, Camilla thought how wonderful it would be to walk forever with Marcus. They went without a word to the top of the bluff, their bluff, and looked down into the dark pool of water.

When he spoke, his voice was gentle. "I'd never think you a wanton, Camilla, or a horrible creature."

He didn't ask about the twins. She could tell him or not.

"They belong to Decimus," she said finally, her voice expressionless. "He collects twin slaves. He took them to Syria with him, but he sent them home about a month ago. They were sick."

"They don't look sick now."

"No." she stared out at the surging water, remembering her revulsion when the cart had pulled up in front of the villa. She'd come out to see. The two little boys had lain curled up together, their bodies entwined. The high hot flush of fever flamed in their faces, but they shuddered with chills. She'd stared down at them. They were terribly ill.

Priscus said impassively, "Shall I have them put in the sick room, my lady?"

She'd glanced at him and realized Priscus hated them, too. Did he fear their influence? She could have agreed and sent them off to die. Then one of the boys opened glazed eyes and stared up at her. She took a breath. "Get the Greek doctor from Neapolis." She'd turned and hurried away from the cart.

"The doctor worked and worked with them," she told Marcus. "Now they are very well."

She didn't look at Marcus. She continued to stare at the dark water and the glitter of phosphorescence as little breakers curved and broke beyond the bay.

Somewhere on the water a ship moved in the night bringing Decimus home.

Camilla sighed and drew her cloak closer. "We'd better start back. It will be dark soon."

"Camilla." He touched her arm and she was painfully aware of the warmth of his hand. "Why did you run away this afternoon?"

"If I'd stayed . . ."

"Yes?"

He must know. She looked up at him, but dusk was truly falling and his face was just a paleness near her. "I wish I could see you clearly."

He moved nearer, so near they almost touched as they faced each other on the cliffside. "Why, Camilla?"

"If I could see your face, then perhaps I'd know what you really think of me."

"What I think of you?" he repeated softly. "Surely that is clear."

He must think she was a woman seeking love, one of the wild young matrons eager to sample all kinds of sensual delights. "I suppose it's clear enough," she said quietly. "You think I can be a plaything, a lover, someone to while away afternoons until someone better comes along."

"No." He gripped her arms roughly. "No, Camilla," he said brusquely. "I don't think that at all." He said haltingly, "I don't know what to think. I've never met anyone like you. I dreamed about you last night. I was trying to swim to you and you were swept farther and farther away. I woke up sweating and half-sick. All I think about is your face and your eyes and how it felt to hold you in my arms. I know that having you in my arms felt right." He paused, said in a rush. "I know you don't know me, but ever since I glimpsed you across the cove I've been like a man possessed. I must know you. Even if it sounds mad and impossible to you, I think you and I belong together."

Camilla stepped back a pace and, reluctantly, he let her go.

"I am married to Decimus." She said flatly, dully. She whirled around and started back up the path.

He caught her in only two strides, pulled her around, and into his arms. His mouth closed over hers, at first gently, then more surely, then fiercely, demandingly, hungrily.

For an instant, Camilla held herself rigid, then she began to kiss him in return. Kisses. She'd never known kisses, never kissed a man. These feelings were new and wonderful and amazing, and there was no time for thought, only feeling. She loved the feel of his mouth, the warmth and intimacy. She clung to him, pressed herself against him and knew, as her breath quickened, that she was experiencing feelings she'd never known.

A faint shout sounded, invading this moment. She didn't want to heed anything but the warmth of Marcus. The cry came again. "Camilla, Camilla."

Camilla pulled away. "We can't. We mustn't."

His hands slipped down on her hips, tugging her close to him, and she yielded, welcoming the pressure of his body.

Nearer now, a high voice called, "Camilla, where are you?"

Camilla pushed against Marcus's chest. "That's Phoebe," she said breathlessly. "Let me go."

"I don't want to ever let you go."

"She's coming." Camilla stepped away and turned to walk up the path, her mind and body aflame with unexpected sensations.

Phoebe came around a curve of the bluff. "Oh, Mistress, there you are." She spoke hurriedly, with a glance over her shoulder. "Priscus is coming with a torch to show you the way home."

Camilla drew her breath in, suddenly alert and wary. Priscus cared nothing for her safety or convenience. He was coming with a torch to spy and Phoebe, clever Phoebe, sensed she might need a warning. Was her attraction to Marcus that obvious? Or only to eyes that knew her well? She knew her face was flushed and her gown rumpled. But the wind was up and Priscus couldn't see her that clearly in torchlight. She continued to walk up the path, but she was achingly aware of Marcus close behind her.

Tonight she'd intended to make it clear to Marcus that she

wasn't a dallier, that he could look to other married women for desire in the afternoon.

But his mouth had drawn and held her. How could she escape him now?

VI

"Camilla, what's all this bustling about?" The senator waved a hand at figures moving rapidly, purposefully in the courtyard.

"Good morning, Papa. Did the noise wake you?"

Her father shook his head. "I've been up since first light and taken a walk. What's the excitement about?"

"I've decided to go back to Rome today."

"Today?" Her father beamed. "Camilla, I can't tell you how much this means to me."

She stared at him for an instant before she understood and felt a rush of embarrassment and sadness. Her father thought she was hurrying back to Rome to talk to Cornelia. Actually, she was running away from Marcus, from the touch of his hands and the warmth of his mouth.

"I know you can reach Cornelia, persuade her to be the fine matron she should be," her father continued.

"I'll do my best, Papa." With that she knew she was committed to talk to Cornelia. Yet with the memory of Marcus's body against hers, what could she say? But talk to her sister she must.

"When do you leave, Camilla?"

"Within the hour. I'm sorry to miss the rest of your visit. Do stay as long as you wish."

"I will stay for awhile. It's a pleasure to be here. As I walked along the colonnade, I almost thought I saw your mother waiting for me in the shadows."

Camilla nodded. "I feel her presence here, too, Papa. It must be because she was happy here." She slipped her hand through her father's arm and they walked companionably out into the courtyard.

"Will Decimus come here or to Rome?"

"I'll send word that I'm in Rome," Camilla replied and she was proud that her voice didn't change. "We need to be in Rome anyway for Terentia's wedding."

Her father plunged into a happy discussion of the wedding plans. "I believe I'll ask your Aunt Lollia to join their hands together."

At a wedding, a matron who had been married only once was chosen to put the bride's hand into the groom's.

"She'll be pleased, Papa."

"I would choose you, Camilla, but I want you to take your mother's place."

"I can't take her place," Camilla said softly, "but I'll be glad to stand by Terentia."

Her father gave her a quick hug. "If Terentia can be as wonderful a wife as you are, Camilla, then . . ."

"Don't say that," Camilla cut in sharply.

Her father looked at her in surprise. "But, Camilla, I only want everything to go as well for Terentia as it has for you."

"Let's hope Terentia has her own happiness, Papa. I don't think it's wise to wish one person's life for another."

And the gods willing, Camilla thought, Terentia would never know the misery she'd experienced.

"I didn't know you were superstitious," her father chided. "You've spent too much time among women while Decimus has been gone."

Camilla shrugged. Let her father think her superstitious. It was infinitely better than that he should know the truth. But if she never told him about Decimus, she could never be free for only her father could obtain her divorce. So many of her friends were divorced. Their fathers were eager to please their daughters, and eager, too, to regain control of handsome dowries.

Perhaps this was the moment to tell her father.

He clapped her on the shoulder. "Have a good journey, Camilla. You'll probably be on your way before I get back from Tiberius's stable. He's going to let me ride that brood mare of his. We may be able to work out a deal." He laughed. "D'you know, I feel years younger here at the villa." Then he was striding away, looking so much stronger than when he arrived, robust, eager, almost like a boy in his desire to be outdoors and astride a horse.

Camilla didn't call him back. This wasn't the moment. What good would it do? It was madness to think he'd ever approve a divorce. She knew how he felt about married women who fell in love with men other than their husbands. She was going to do the right thing. She was going back to Rome without a word to Marcus. What would he think of her? That she was fickle? Insensitive? Callous? Her heart ached. She couldn't say goodbye to him. If he came near, if he touched her, she would be lost.

The only solution was to make a clean break. Leave Swallow's Nest. Run back to Rome and ready the house for Decimus's return. Immerse herself in the social life, the theater, the races, visits with her friends, literary readings and banquets, the Baths, the libraries.

Walking with her down every street would be a memory, a memory of strength and power and grace, a memory of a man with curly black hair and bright dark eyes, young, determined, virile. But memory can't feed on itself. Ultimately, the memories would fade, grow dim. She might even see Marcus one day at the law courts or the Forum and nod and smile brightly and pass him without a pang.

Only her heart would know.

She'd never before cared for anyone. She'd never experienced the rush of feelings that swept her when she was in Marcus's arms. She'd known that love was real. Her parents' steadfast devotion to each other had been her guide, but the glory of touch and sense had not been hers. This brief and vivid moment would be all she'd ever realize of love. She knew, without being told, that she'd barely tasted of love, that there were joys and delights she'd never even imagined, could not now imagine.

Phoebe hurried down the steps from the house. "Everything is packed, but Priscus wants to know if the twins are to come."

"No." Short, clipped, definite.

Phoebe ducked nearer. "Maybe you should take them. Won't Decimus want them?"

"If he wants them, he can send for them. Tell Priscus he is to stay here."

But Priscus himself loomed up behind Phoebe. He bowed deferentially. "I'm sorry, my lady. I wish I could stay here. After all, it's hot in Rome now. But the Master told me specifically to accompany you on all journeys." He spread his hands in mock helplessness. "Much as I appreciate your thoughtfulness, I'll have to come to Rome, too."

Camilla shrugged indifferently. "Whatever you wish, Priscus." She turned on her heel. The hated Priscus would still be underfoot. But she wouldn't have to listen to the high giggles of the twins. At least, not until Decimus returned.

Perhaps his ship would sink.

How horrid to think such a thing, she thought sharply. To wish ill for a ship full of innocent travelers. She made a little prayer to Mercury for their safety because she mustn't let her dislike of Decimus twist her mind and spirit.

It took longer to set off than she'd hoped. It was four hours after sunrise before the long train of litters and wagons got underway. Even at a rapid pace, it would take almost a week to reach Rome. The best litter carriers could manage only twenty miles a day.

Camilla rested back against soft silk cushions as her litter began to jolt down the avenue. She didn't look back at the villa. It was the first time in her life she'd left without a farewell glance. Always, the villa had been her favorite place, her happy place. This past year, without Decimus, she'd gloried in the sea-salt air and the rugged cliff paths and the heady sense of freedom. Now, she lay in her litter, staring sternly at the horizon, trying not to remember that shocking moment when she'd plummeted through the air and sunk beneath the cold water—and the warmth and strength of the hands that had saved her.

Each night, she and her company stopped at a friend's villa. The slaves were put up in quarters and she was welcomed with glad cries and fed marvelous meals and made much of.

"So Decimus is coming home. We'll have to plan a celebration . . ."

"Are you excited about the wedding? Tell us all about it."

"Here, Camilla, meet our newest baby. Isn't he just the image of his father?"

The third night, she stayed at the seaside villa of her old friends Quintilia and Servius Tullius. As they were entering the dining room, a slave announced, "Another guest is arriving, Master."

Servius looked up and raised a hand in greeting. "Marcus, old man, are you on your way back to Rome so soon?"

Camilla looked, too, and was shaken by the strength of feeling that swept her, the joy and delight and excitement.

Quintilia turned to Camilla. “Marcus is an old friend of ours. He was through here last month on his way to his father’s new estate.” Her face wrinkled. “I believe it’s not far from your villa.”

“Marcus is our new neighbor,” Camilla said. “We’ve met.” What simple words to mark the most dramatic moment of her life.

“Isn’t he a darling?” Quintilia said cheerfully. “It’s too bad we already have husbands. A girl could fall in love with Marcus.”

“I imagine that’s true,” Camilla replied.

Servius was delighted at Marcus’s arrival. “I thought the seaside would be too quiet for you, Marc.”

Marcus looked at Camilla. “I didn’t find it too quiet. But Rome has more attractions now.”

“More pretty girls,” Servius boomed. “But we have a beautiful guest with us tonight. Marcus, why don’t you share a couch with Camilla?”

“I’d like that.”

Camilla didn’t look at him as they took their places. The cushion between them accentuated his nearness. She could hear the light sound of his breathing. He was so near.

The first course of oysters and deviled eggs was followed by baked trout with a thick sweet sauce and fresh asparagus. The meal ended with apple fritters and sharp, dry Falernian wine mixed with water. As they drank the wine, Marcus and Servius discussed a case Servius was going to argue next month.

Quintilia turned to Camilla. “You’re quiet this evening.” Her observant eyes flickered toward Marcus.

Camilla gave a little shrug. “I suppose it’s the travel.”

“Why are you going back to Rome so early? You know how hot it is. No one will be in town.”

Camilla knew Marcus was listening. "I need to help my father plan Terentia's wedding."

"Oh, is Terentia getting married? Why didn't you tell me? That's wonderful. I want to hear all about it." Quintilia was really excited when she learned of the bridegroom-to-be. "A sister of his is a very good friend of mine. Is the date set yet?"

Camilla made sensible answers and somehow managed not to look toward Marcus. Finally, dinner ended and Servius invited them to walk down to his lake.

Camilla and Quintilia followed the men down a tree-shaded path. Quintilia whispered, "Servius is so proud of the lake. He had it built in the spring and the overseer did a remarkable job."

They stopped on a short rise overlooking the shallow lake. Servius waved his hand, describing the basketloads of dirt the slaves dug away to make the shallow basin and how he'd devised a dam downstream to backup the water.

Marcus clapped his friend on the shoulder. "You enjoy your villa more than anyone I know."

Servius's laugh boomed again. "I'll bet you think it's funny, Marc, to see me so domesticated. I know you never thought I'd be a good husband and father. But it's easy. All you need is the right woman," and he reached out and pulled Quintilia close.

"Now, Servius," Quintilia scolded, but her eyes shone with pleasure.

"I guarantee the married life, Marcus. It's time we found a wife for you."

Marcus didn't smile. He looked soberly at his friend. "I'd hoped to find a wife when I came home from Greece."

"That's no problem," Servius responded. "We'll have some parties, invite all the pretty girls."

"No. I know who I want."

Servius looked interested. "Who is she, old man?"

Marcus just shook his head. "I'll tell you when I win her." He pointed to several gaily-colored punts moored alongside a wooden dock. "Can we take a row?"

"Sure."

The foursome walked down to the dock. Marcus smiled, "Do you want to take your wife out, Servius?"

"Gladly."

Marcus turned to Camilla. "Would you like to go out on the water?"

"That would be very nice."

He held her arm to help her down into the punt. He took his place opposite her and picked up the pole and edged the punt away from the dock.

Neither of them spoke.

Camilla leaned over the side and trailed her hand through the cool water.

"Camilla."

Slowly, reluctantly, she looked at him, uncertain what she would find in his eyes. Anger? Dislike? Disdain? Tears pricked her eyes.

"Why are you crying?" he asked gently.

She shook her head.

Marcus began to pull swiftly and the punt skimmed across the water, farther and farther away from Servius and Quintilia.

"You ran away from me again."

Camilla nodded.

"It won't do any good," he said decidedly. "You can't escape me. I've known you were meant for me ever since I first saw you standing on the bluff." He paused and spoke so softly the words caressed her. "You were lovely. The wind molded your dress against you. I came back every evening, hoping to have a glimpse of you. Then that night when you didn't come, I went ahead into the water. I was halfway toward shore when I saw you walk to the place where I'd dived and I knew you must have seen me, too, those other times. Then you fell." He reached over and took her hand and his fingers gripped hers, hard and warm, live and vibrant.

She stared at him and knew her eyes revealed her heart.

"You care," Marcus said vigorously.

Slowly, she nodded.

"You're going to be mine." His tone was utterly confident.

"I would like to kiss you," she said softly. "Once more. Just once more."

"Not once. A hundred times, a thousand. You and I are meant to share our kisses forever."

"No, Marcus."

His face was abruptly dark as a stormy sky. "Why not?"

"I am Decimus's wife."

Marcus jammed the pole against the bottom and the punt jerked forward. "I hate hearing you say that. But I accept it. It's a fact. You are his wife at this moment, but we will talk to him. Surely, he will give you a divorce if you ask, if you tell him about how we feel."

"I can't ask him," she said dully.

"Do you love him?" There was despair in his voice.

"I hate him."

Marcus looked bewildered. "If that's the case, there's no reason not to leave him. We'll talk to Decimus."

"He will never give me a divorce."

"Your father can demand it."

Tears slipped down her cheeks. "My father opposes divorce. Under any circumstances."

Marcus was explosive. "If he knew how unhappy you were, surely he'd help you get free."

Camilla shook her head. "My father considers marriage a bond forever."

"We'll talk to Decimus," Marcus insisted. "No man would want to hold a woman who doesn't love him."

"Decimus will. My lands are too important to him."

"He would hold you against your will?

"Yes." She brushed away the tears and looked unhappily at Marcus. "You see, there's no future for us. I'll never be free."

"I won't settle for that," Marcus said roughly. "I won't leave you locked in a foul marriage." He looked at her intently. "Because there's much you haven't told me about Decimus. Isn't there?"

"It would serve no purpose," she said quietly.

Marcus's face hardened. "Perhaps it's as well you haven't told me. I might not be able to keep my hands off his throat."

"Marcus," her voice was gentle, defeated, "you mustn't worry about me. I can manage. I've managed for a long time."

His face was stern. "I'm going to talk to Decimus."

"No."

"Camilla, if I don't, we'll never be together."

She scrubbed tears off her face, awkwardly, as a child might. How could she be having this conversation? She and Marcus scarcely knew each other but their moments together had created a bond that she knew could endure for a lifetime, a lifetime of learning about each other, loving each other. "Marcus," she said huskily, "I know that there could be a great love between us. But I love my father. I owe him my life. I can't break his heart."

Marcus's shoulders slumped. He stared at her, his dark eyes pleading.

She shook her head, slowly, with finality.

He lifted the pole and jammed it into the lakebed and the punt moved back toward shore. As it slipped by a man-made island, they were screened from view.

"Marcus, stop for just a moment."

He plunged the pole down. The punt rocked, then steadied.

She reached across the space between them to touch his cheeks with her hands. "I wish we could have loved, Marcus. I wish it more than I've ever wished for anything in this world." She leaned forward and kissed him. For a wonderful moment, their lips touched gently and tenderly, lightly as the wings of a butterfly brush a sweet flower. Camilla sank back onto her seat. "We'd better go in now."

Marcus poled the punt swiftly across the water. When he helped her up onto the dock, he held her hand tightly once more and said, "Camilla, we have only one life to live. You'll have to decide whether to live it for yourself or for others."

VII

Traffic thickened as they neared the outskirts of Rome. Camilla left the curtain of her litter open to catch what little breeze moved across the dusty countryside. A cohort of soldiers marched past. Carts rumbled by, hurrying to Rome to be ready to enter after sundown to make deliveries of bricks or vegetables or olive oil. The clop of mule hooves, the shriek of ungreased axles, the cymbals of a foreign religious procession gave a taste of the noise that would greet them in Rome itself. Camilla rerolled her scroll of poems. It was impossible to read amidst the clangor. But, if she didn't read, she would think. She didn't want to think. Her thoughts ran in a familiar groove, love or duty, duty or love. Self or family. Marcus or her father. Whom would she love and honor?

Marcus had left very early the next morning from Servius's villa. She hadn't seen him after their farewell at the lake. It wasn't any good thinking about Marcus. That was over before it began. Marcus could look for a wife among the many beautiful girls in Rome.

Miserable, Camilla unrolled the scroll. Her eyes fell on a snatch of poetry. "Kiss quickly for the days of summer fly away, then comes the winter of the heart."

If she remained true to her father's precepts, she must turn away from Marcus. If she didn't . . . For an instant, Camilla let herself remember the feel of Marcus's mouth. Love could be hers for the taking.

How could she choose a path that would break her father's heart?

The litter-bearers swung over the rise of a hill and Camilla saw the faraway glisten of marble that was Rome. She was almost home.

The excitement of nearing Rome infected her train. The litter-bearers picked up their pace. The slave boys prodded the donkeys to a trot. They crossed the Appian bridge over the Tiber and swung past a sprawling bath complex and the Temple of Virtue, the Temple of Diana.

Noise echoed and re-echoed from the walls of buildings as they plunged into the narrow, twisting streets. It was almost noon and a last frenzy seized workmen and vendors before food and siesta time.

By law, the carts in Camilla's train had to wait at the city gates until sundown to lessen traffic on the crowded streets, but her litter was free because of her station in society to worm its way through the throngs. They passed the street of the blacksmiths with all its heat and clanging, then, blessed quiet, turned up a street of booksellers where slaves sat and copied the latest manuscripts. They curved past the center of Rome, the Forum. The law courts sat empty now under the heavy summer sun. They would resume their business in September. Government clerks, slaves, and foreigners crowded the narrow streets. The crowd thinned as they neared the Aventine Hill and began the steep climb past lovely mansions surrounded by green parks.

Their house sat near the crown of the hill. It was one of the finest in all of Rome. She and Decimus had bought it soon after their marriage through the sale of three of Camilla's farms.

The previous owner had to open his veins because the Emperor accused him of complicity in a conspiracy. Phoebe had shuddered when she told Camilla that the former master bled to death in the garden near a marble statue of Diana. No one dared oppose the Emperor. Camilla felt a chill despite the hot afternoon. She never walked to that part of the garden.

It was a magnificent mansion, Camilla thought, as her bearers lowered the litter for her to get out. Phoebe stood by to help her mistress.

The overseer of the Aventine house hurried out to greet her. "Welcome home, Mistress. Everything is in readiness for you."

"Thank you, Pharmaces. I know you've taken good care of everything."

Camilla felt weary from the journey, but she must inspect the house or the staff would be disappointed. Pharmaces proudly led her through the rooms. The reception hall smelled of fresh paint. The ornately carved wooden columns glowed a bright red and the frescoes on the east wall had been retouched. Fresh gold and green paint gleamed in the study and red again brightened the colonnade around the courtyard. Finally, however, she'd seen everything, even the spotless kitchen. She smiled and dismissed Pharmaces.

Her financial adviser, Justus, waited in the study to give her the latest report on her properties and investments. He smiled happily. "If I may say so, Miss Camilla, we've done well this year. Very, very well. A two-fold increase in profits."

"That's marvelous, Justus." She tried hard to sound delighted for his sake. Obviously, he'd worked very hard. What ultimate difference did greater wealth make, Camilla wondered. The increased income would please Decimus, of course. But pleasing

Decimus hadn't mattered to her for a long, long time. When Justus left, his face still wreathed in smiles, Camilla walked moodily around the study. She felt caged, imprisoned.

Phoebe said brightly, "Shall I ready your room, Miss Camilla? Would you like to nap?"

It was the siesta hour. All Rome would be quiet now, heavy pulsing sunlight bathing the streets except for those perpetually dim from the five- and six-story apartment houses looming above the narrow streets.

Camilla shook her head at Phoebe and walked restlessly back toward the reception hall. Gold and ivory intertwined in the intricate reliefs on the ceilings. The mosaic floor glittered cheerfully in the sunlight streaming down through the central opening in the roof. Water bubbled in the tiled pool.

Camilla stopped in front of a bust of Decimus. The sculpture was a good likeness, capturing the sly curve of his sensuous mouth, his heavy-lidded eyes and high, almost oriental cheekbones.

She whirled away from the bust and paced down the hall and back into the study and through it to the steps leading down into the courtyard. This courtyard was smaller than the one at the villa, of course, but beautifully designed with box hedges, rosemary, damask roses, lilies, violets, and sweet rocket. The late August sun steamed overhead. Heat pressed against the vivid greenery. Camilla felt boxed in and wished for the villa. There, she could walk out into the park and stride, alone and free, along the bluff and look out at the dark blue water and feel the sweep of salty air on her face.

"Come, Miss Camilla, why don't you take a siesta?" Phoebe urged.

Camilla knew Phoebe meant well, but the idea of resting in her small darkened room increased her claustrophobic feeling.

Returning to Rome hadn't solved anything. She'd carried her

feelings of despair with her. She'd told Marcus they could not be together. Ahead lay empty barren years with nothing to ease her heartbreak. But she'd made her decision. Divorce was out of the question, and she wasn't going to become one of the matrons whose escapades titillated Rome. Like her sister.

She turned to Phoebe. "Call my litter. I'm going to the Baths." She might be imprisoned in Rome, but she didn't have to stay at the house.

Camilla sweltered in her jolting litter. The afternoon sun scourged the city. Most wealthy Romans fled the city in the summers to the coolness of the mountains or sea. The big public baths would be jammed with those who couldn't afford a journey or who didn't have villas to visit. Camilla directed her bearers to a small, exclusive bath complex in the Campius Martius. She'd be more likely to find someone she knew at the smaller, private bath.

She felt better the minute she entered the section of the bath reserved for women. Bright green tiles felt cool underfoot. On the walls of the dressing area, a painted forest on the walls beckoned to deep and green coolness with painted ivy twining thickly. Brightly painted birds looked so lifelike she almost expected them to sing.

Her slave girl, Antonia, helped her disrobe. Camilla walked past the steam room. Surely it was hot enough in Rome this afternoon to forego a steam bath. A whiff of moist air wafted out of the hot room. Camilla hurried on to the cold-water plunge. Octopi and sea serpents and bulging-eyed fish swarmed in blue watered frescoes. Only two other women were in the plunge.

Camilla bent down to touch the cold water. Quickly, she slipped over the side. The coldness made her gasp. She began to swim, stroking slowly down the length of the pool, the water smooth against her body. Unencumbered by her heavy dress, she felt as light and swift as a fish. Rolling over on her back, she looked up at the immense vaulted ceiling and the cool greens and blues and blacks melded into a stream of soothing color.

Finally, the cold ached in her bones. She swam to the side and pulled herself up out of the water, shivering. She nodded hello to the other women. One's figure curved in voluptuous folds. The other was too thin. But Camilla saw their wedding rings. Matrons, both of them. It was odd. Three women sharing for a moment the same sensations, the hot steamy afternoon, the aching coldness of the plunge. But she knew their bodies had felt sensations she'd never shared.

Abruptly, she stood and walked back to the main hallway. She was terribly cold now. She'd spent too long in the cold-water plunge. She hurried into the warm room and found it to herself. She stepped down into the small square basin filled with warm water, smooth and soft as milk. It rose up and covered the long paleness that was her body.

Camilla sank gratefully onto a stone bench. Warm water eddied around her, silky and caressing. This pool was so different from the cold plunge. And so different from the dark water of the cove where she would have sunk forever except for the strong grip of Marcus's hands. Marcus's hands . . . She looked at the shimmering gleam of her body through the milky green water. Marcus's hands . . . What would it feel like . . .

"Camilla, I didn't know you were back in Rome."

Startled, Camilla looked up. Julia Calvus stood beside the basin. She stretched like a sleepy cat. She had round and perfect breasts and a flat stomach and slim legs. She dropped lightly into the water beside Camilla.

"You looked a hundred leagues away, Camilla."

Julia was extremely perceptive as are so many unhappy people. Camilla certainly didn't want Julia to have any inkling what she'd been thinking.

"Enjoying the warm water, Julia."

"What are you doing in Rome?"

"I need to help Papa with the plans for Terentia's wedding. I'm surprised to see you. I thought you were on your way to Baiae when you stopped by the villa."

"We were, but Lucius received word of some ship or other that went down. He was all in a swivet. We had to come back. It's a terrible bore." Then she smiled, a satisfied, secret smile. "I don't mind being back in Rome."

Camilla didn't have to ask. It would be a man, of course.

Julia's eyes darkened, looked hot and shiny.

Camilla looked away.

Julia laughed, a low, husky, wanton laugh. "Camilla, don't you ever get a little weary of being so perfect?"

Stung, Camilla faced her. "Perfect? What do you mean?"

"Perfect, my dear." Julia's voice was edged by disdain. "Camilla Scipio Rufini, the most beautiful and perfect matron in all of Rome. So rich. So intelligent. So beautiful. So respected. Obedient to her father, faithful to her husband." Julia slapped the water. "Tell me, Camilla, this past year, with Decimus gone, didn't you once, just once, make love to a man?"

The words hung between them in the warm air.

Slowly, Camilla shook her head.

Julia arched an eyebrow. "What's wrong with you? Do you have ice instead of blood in your veins? Didn't you want someone?"

Did she want someone?

"Ahh," Julia crowed. "Not a word from you. So the perfect Camilla does have stirrings in her loins. Let me tell you, my dear, the answer is easy. Take a lover."

Camilla pushed away from the bench, but the splash of the water didn't drown out the throaty laughter that followed. As warm, silky water flowed against her, Camilla thought of

Marcus. He had pulled her hard against him when they stood on the bluff after the dinner for her father. What would it be like to love him?

Camilla came to the end of the basin and, reluctantly, turned to float back. Julia waited, still smiling. When she reached the other end, Julia said mockingly, "Camilla, I believe you're about to learn what life's all about."

Camilla looked up at Julia for a long moment.

Slowly, Julia's smile slipped away and her eyes looked huge and sorrowful.

"I'm not sure," Camilla said quietly, "I really want to know what life is all about."

For an instant, Julia's eyes glistened, then she smiled again, a brittle, determined smile. "What's life? Who knows? I only know it lasts such a little while and no one really cares. You might as well enjoy it. Eat and make love. We'll all be old soon enough. That's all there is." Her smile broadened and it was as though the tiny moment of pain had never been. "Have I told you about my latest lover? Oh, he's a wonder. A prick as big as a mountain, I swear, and when he . . ."

Camilla listened patiently. She knew all about love or what passed for love in Rome. But only from the words of others and, so often, they were tawdry, cheapening words.

Another friend of Julia's wandered in, a fat, hard-faced matron about thirty. When she and Julia began to compare their latest lovers, Camilla excused herself. "I believe I'll take another plunge in the cold water."

She was almost to the door when Julia called out, "Oh Camilla, I swear everyone's back from the coast. When I arrived at the Baths, I saw Marcus Paulus, your new neighbor."

Camilla's chest ached. "Is he here at the baths? Now?"

Julia nodded. "Did you know he was coming to Rome?"

"Oh yes." Camilla spoke casually, carelessly. "I saw him while I was traveling."

"He's a beauty, Camilla. I'll tell you what, when you have a party and invite him, be sure and ask us."

"I will," Camilla said, her voice thin. Marcus wouldn't have a chance if Julia decided to have him. Abruptly, painfully, she pictured the two of them together, Julia's slender body and Marcus's strong, firm body. An indescribable sense of anguish and loss swept her. But she had no right to care what Marcus did. And he was a man. There would be women. If she turned him away, there would be women, and, ultimately, a wife. Someone he could join in the night, holding near, kissing gently or fiercely, over and over and over again.

Camilla walked out into the hall. Marcus was in the baths now. He would be out in the great open courtyard in the men's huge cold-water plunge.

Camilla walked faster and faster toward the women's cold-water plunge. One day last winter, when she and Julia had lolled desultorily in the warm water basin, Julia told her of a tiny gap in a wall of the women's cold-water plunge. The small opening was in an alcove. A rent in the bricks gave a slitted view of the central courtyard and the men's exercise ground and pool. Julia'd laughed her husky, hungry laugh. "If you want to know the truth beneath the togas, Camilla, take a look. Then you'll know which ones are worth the chase."

As always with Julia, Camilla'd been partially entertained and partially disgusted. Of course, Camilla had no intention ever of spying on the men.

Camilla nodded hello to several women in the shallow end of the cold-water plunge. She dived in and slowly swam the length of the pool. Once again the cold shook her, reminding her of the deep pool in the rocky cove and Marcus, always Marcus. She stopped at the far end of the pool and held onto the side. She could see the alcove.

Slowly, she pulled herself out of the pool and, shivering, stepped into the alcove. Once hidden by its curving walls, she stepped up onto a concrete bench and found the opening, a pale, oblong blob in the darkness of the bricks.

Two fat, balding men lounged on some nearby steps. A group of boys played tag. Some young men casually tossed a huge ball around a circle. Camilla's eyes skimmed over their nakedness without interest. Then she saw Marcus in the pool. He swam powerfully, his arms driving through the water, his legs beating rhythmically. He reached the end and pulled himself out of the water. The sun glistened on his body, touching his skin with gold. He turned and Camilla saw him full figure, his tousled dark hair and bold face, his powerful arms and chest, his lean, muscular legs.

She gripped the uneven bricks of the wall. Desire and a wild excitement swept her. Both of them stood naked, so young and alive. But with a wall between them.

Priscus bowed deferentially.

Camilla looked up from the scroll she was reading. For an instant longer, Horace's sonorous words echoed in her mind; then she came back to the present, the shadowy coolness of the library, the quiet of an August afternoon. "Yes, Priscus?"

"A letter from the Master." He handed her the tablet.

She laid it on the table top. Priscus bowed again and softly walked away. She hadn't heard him coming. Camilla stared after him thoughtfully. He moved so quietly and he watched her so closely.

Her gaze dropped to the marble-topped table and the tablet. Slowly, she rolled up the scroll, laid it down and picked up the tablet.

"My dearest Camilla,

"By the time this reaches you, I should be within a week's journey of Rome. I will go to the house in Rome, as I must make arrangements about a matter of vital importance."

Camilla frowned. A matter of vital importance. She skimmed the rest of the message. "*. . . heard Cornelia and her husband are favorites at the Palace . . . I'm pleased the crop forecast for our farms is so good . . .*"

But the final paragraph shocked her.

"Should you hear ugly rumors of my activities, don't be distressed. I have enemies who wish to prevent my becoming consul next year. I know, with your strong support, all will be well."

Camilla looked through the open archway into the reception hall. The bust of Decimus was in shadow, but she didn't need to see the sculpture to remember his face, his dark and clever and somewhat dangerous face.

What had Decimus done?

His uncharacteristic personal plea indicated he must be under great stress, because she and Decimus didn't share confidences. How would her support help him? She shrugged. She didn't really care what he'd done.

She frowned. But he was her husband. His actions reflected upon her family. How dreadful it would be if Decimus were involved in something truly disgraceful. How upsetting for her father.

There was no point in worrying about his problems now. Likely he needed money. And she had plenty of money.

The most disturbing news was that Decimus would be back within the week. Her father would also come back to Rome this week to complete plans for Terentia's wedding and she had yet to talk to Cornelia. She couldn't put that meeting off any longer. Today seemed to be a day for disagreeable tasks.

Camilla called for her litter. It wasn't far to Cornelia and Titus's house. They lived on the opposite side of the Aventine Hill. It was odd, in a way, that the sisters saw little of each other despite living so near. But what Camilla had told her father was true. She and Decimus were not included among those who spent much of their time at the Palace, though she knew Decimus wished they did. She always tried to avoid dining at Cornelia's because she didn't like Cornelia's husband. Titus could be very charming, but Camilla didn't like the sardonic tone in his voice or the cold look in his eyes. Titus ignored women at banquets. He always cornered bankers and travelers and was rude and indifferent to senators with modest holdings. If anyone loved money and power more than Decimus, it was Titus. It wouldn't surprise Camilla to learn Cornelia's marriage was floundering. Though what Papa expected her to say to Cornelia, she couldn't imagine. But she had to make the effort.

Camilla rehearsed a dozen beginnings as the litter jolted through the streets. She still didn't know what she was going to say when she walked into Cornelia's room.

One slave worked with Cornelia's hair, piling the lovely dark-red tresses in a delicate upswept style that emphasized the graceful line of Cornelia's neck. Another slave held a jewel case in front of her mistress. Cornelia stared intently at the jewelry, fingering a heavy pearl necklace, then lifting up pendant earrings with pearls big as gooseberries.

"Cornelia."

Cornelia looked around. For an instant, her face was utterly blank, then she jumped up from her chair and rushed to greet Camilla.

As they embraced, Camilla smelled the sweetness of rose perfume and the freshness of Cornelia's hair and gown.

"When did you get back to Rome?" Cornelia asked excitedly.

"A few days ago. I've been seeing to the house. Decimus is on his way home."

"How nice for you, Camilla."

Cornelia's response showed how far apart the sisters had grown.

"And, of course, we have to get ready for Terentia's wedding," Camilla said briskly, not wanting to talk about Decimus.

"Terentia's wedding?" Cornelia repeated blankly. She stared at Camilla out of green eyes that looked suddenly huge and vulnerable. "Is Terentia getting married?"

Numbly, Camilla nodded. It had never occurred to her that her father hadn't informed Cornelia.

"How did you know, Camilla?"

Camilla looked at the frescoe on the opposite wall, at a bright blue expanse of water and high-masted ships and palm trees and tigers. "I'm sure Papa will come tell you. He isn't in Rome right now. I suppose he just hasn't had a chance to send word."

Cornelia turned away from Camilla. She waved her hand at the waiting slaves. "Leave us."

The hairdresser and attendant hurried away. When they were alone, Cornelia faced Camilla. She lifted her chin and Camilla was struck by her beauty. Her sister was lovely, her gentle sensitive face and rich red hair and the long perfect line of her throat.

"Cornelia, you are strikingly beautiful," Camilla exclaimed.

Cornelia's mouth twisted. "I wish I'd been born with a humped back and stringy hair and a lumpy face."

Camilla drew in a shocked breath. "How can you say that?"

"I am beautiful." Cornelia's voice was empty. "Beauty has brought me nothing but grief."

Camilla stared at her sister in dismay.

"Now," Cornelia said unhappily, "Papa doesn't even come to tell me my little sister will be married." Tears glistened in her eyes. "Ah well, it doesn't matter. I'd probably be too busy to be a part of her happiness."

"No, Cornelia. Of course you'll come to the wedding. How do you suppose Terentia would feel if you stayed away?"

Cornelia's lips quivered, then she said lightly, "I'll probably come. I can tell Terentia a lot about marriage."

Camilla said quickly, "She's marrying a nice boy. A Pompidae from Pompeii."

Cornelia smiled, but it wasn't a pleasant smile. "A Pompidae from Pompeii. Papa succeeds again. Perhaps this will be the best marriage of all. For his purposes. Well, I hope Terentia's marriage is better than mine. And I hope Papa has his fill of Titus being such a favorite of the Emperor's. I wonder if it would please Papa to know why Titus is so influential?"

The bitter edge to Cornelia's voice frightened Camilla. "Cornelia, please. Don't be angry."

Cornelia stared at her, her cheeks patched with red. "You and Papa see so much of each other. Perhaps you'd like to tell him why the Emperor favors Titus?"

"Cornelia, don't be angry with me. I love you. Papa loves you."

Cornelia shook her head. "Papa doesn't love me. He was proud of me, proud of my beauty. Because I look like Mother. But I haven't turned out to be a fine Roman matron like Mother." Her eyes narrowed. "Is that why you've come, my noble sister? Did Papa send you to ask about my wanton ways?"

So it was true, the story Papa overheard in the baths. Camilla stared at her lovely sister in dismay. How could Cornelia with her regal bearing involve herself with gladiators, the most brutal and vicious men in Rome? How could she bear to be touched by any of them?

"I see it in your face," Cornelia said angrily. "You've come to tell me about the old Roman virtues. Papa is so fond of those virtues," she said sarcastically. "He so admires Rome and Romans. Then I'm sure it will thrill him to know I've bedded the Emperor. You may tell him, Camilla. His daughter has lain with a god. You did know that Caligula has decreed that he is a living god?"

Camilla stared at her sister in stricken silence.

Cornelia laughed. The laughter grated in the quiet room. "Oh yes, I've spread my legs for Caligula. Isn't that wonderful?" Her mouth twisted. Tears began to edge down her cheeks.

"Cornelia, why?" Camilla asked huskily.

"Do you think I'm mad? Sometimes I wish I were mad. It would make my life more bearable." She shuddered. "I hate Caligula. I hate for him to touch me. His hands are always sticky. His neck is scrawny and his legs . . . He has little pin legs stuck to a bulging body. He's so pale, white as a water lily, but hairy."

"If you find him so repulsive, why?"

"I told you Titus was his favorite, didn't I? Don't you understand? Caligula wanted me. He saw me at the banquets. I tried to turn him away, but Titus was thrilled."

Titus was willing to barter his wife's body for his career. It didn't surprise Camilla, but it sickened her. "Cornelia, how terrible."

Her sister dropped her face into her hands for a long moment, then lifted her head. "I'm sorry, Camilla, I'm sorry I told you."

"Cornelia, if Papa knew, surely he would demand a divorce."

Cornelia gripped Camilla's arm so hard it hurt. "You mustn't tell him."

"Why not? I can't bear the thought of you being used like this."

Cornelia shook her head with finality. "Titus told me that if I ever tried to get a divorce, he would send the boys to live with his sister in Egypt. He swore I'd never see them again. Camilla, I can't lose my boys. They're all I have."

Every heart can be held hostage if it truly loves. Camilla knew she would keep her sister's secret, because there would be worse pain for Cornelia if the truth came out.

"Cornelia, I'm sorry, I'm dreadfully sorry."

Cornelia picked up a handkerchief and wiped her eyes. "It's all right, Camilla. It isn't your problem. At least you are happily married."

Camilla looked at her sister. Slowly, she shook her head.

Cornelia reached out and touched Camilla's arm. "Am I wrong?"

"There is no love in my house, Cornelia."

Suddenly, Cornelia was the protective older sister. "Is he cruel to you? Does he hurt you?"

Camilla shook her head. "No, nothing like that. Decimus is always polite. He has other interests."

"Oh. If that's the case, look around you. There are plenty of men who will love a married woman."

"I don't want that. I want love."

Cornelia looked at her sadly. "Everyone wants love."

"You can't find love in hidden visits," Camilla objected hotly. "They mean nothing to anyone."

"Everyone wants love," Cornelia repeated. "Even drunken men who paw you at banquets. That's what they're seeking. No one finds it. D'you know why? Love doesn't exist. It's a mirage."

"No," Camilla said definitely. "Love is real. I know love is real."

Slowly Cornelia smiled. "Who is he, Camilla?"

Camilla didn't answer.

"If you love someone," Cornelia said gently, "then love him. Don't let love pass you by. Don't be a fool."

"I can't."

"Why not?"

"Papa . . . It means so much to him that we be like Mother."

Cornelia's face hardened. "We aren't Mother. We don't have the husband she had. We're trapped, you and I, trapped forever with men who don't care about us. Don't be a fool, Camilla."

Running feet sounded and Cornelia's little boys burst into the room.

"Aunt Camilla," Julius cried, "would you like to see my pet cat? Daddy brought him back from Egypt for me."

"And for me," a hoarse little voiced added.

Camilla hugged both boys. "I'd love to see your cat."

In a moment, they returned, Julius holding firmly to a squirmy mass of gray-brown fluff. He thrust the animal toward Camilla. She accepted it gingerly and rubbed behind the creature's ears. The cat began to purr. "What a nice cat," she said warmly.

"Daddy's going to take us to Egypt with him the next time he goes," Fabius said.

Camilla looked over their heads at Cornelia. The rouge stood out on her cheeks in huge red patches. "We'll see, but Grandfather Scipio may take you boys to the north with him to visit Gaul."

"I'd like that," Julius said.

"I want to go to Egypt," Fabius insisted.

"We'll see. Now it's time for you boys to go to the park with Rufus," Cornelia said, shooing them away.

The boys hugged their mother and Camilla, took the cat, and ran out of the room.

"I won't permit them to go to Egypt without me. And I'm not leaving Rome," Cornelia said determinedly.

Camilla frowned. "How can you prevent Titus from taking them?"

"He likes being a favorite of the Emperor."

Camilla looked away from her sister. Titus bartered his wife's body and now Cornelia bartered it, too. She would do thus and so if Titus met her demands about her sons.

Cornelia said brokenly, "Don't despise me, Camilla."

Camilla bit her lip. "Cornelia, I love you. But I hate seeing you live like this."

"It doesn't really matter," Cornelia said wearily. Then she said softly, so softly Camilla could scarcely hear, "I loved Titus so much when we were first married. I loved him so much. Now, I hate being in the same room with him. At night, I drink too much wine and then it doesn't hurt so much." Her mouth trembled. "Do you remember when we were little and we talked about being grown and having our own houses and how we thought we'd live like Papa and Mother?" Cornelia shook her head, as if shaking away pain and memory. She began to fumble in her jewel box. "Here, I believe I'll wear this one. Will you fasten it, Camilla?"

Camilla came up behind her sister and took the heavy pearl necklace and slipped it around Cornelia's neck and closed the silver clasp.

"Thank you, Camilla. I've certainly enjoyed seeing you again," she said brightly, "but you've caught me dressing to go out. I need to hurry now or I'll be late."

"Late? Where are you going?"

Cornelia retouched her makeup in a silver mirror. "To the baths."

She didn't invite Camilla to come. She reached up and

smoothed her hair, so intricately done. Gold dust glittered against vividly red curls.

Cornelia wasn't going to the baths, Camilla thought. Cornelia was going to meet her lover.

VIII

"Did you have a good journey?" Camilla asked politely.

"Passable. But it's worth the hours of travel to be home. And to see you, my dear," Decimus replied.

They stood in the reception hall. Sunlight flooded down through the square opening in the ceiling. Tiny marble chips, pink and green and rusty red, glittered brightly in the terrazzo floor. Brightly painted marble busts, ranged in the hall, looked lifelike and attentive.

Camilla gazed at her husband appraisingly. He was thinner. That made his face more pointed than ever, sharp nose, sharp chin. As always, he was close shaven, his skin smooth as a boy's. Camilla didn't like to think about that. But there was something different about Decimus's attention to her, this first morning home. Camilla tried to define the difference in the polite pauses between their speaking. Before he left for Syria, he was courteous to her, even genial in an aloof, disinterested fashion. This morning he watched her intently. It was not the loving gaze of a long-separated mate. Indeed, there was something calculating, almost sinister, in his penetrating stare.

Suddenly, he seemed to realize the intensity of his attitude and began to look around the hall. “Everything looks marvelous. I like the way the walls have been repainted.”

“Pharmaces found a very talented Greek artist, a slave of our next-door neighbor,” Camilla explained.

“His owner permits him to work for others?”

“The owner gets a percentage of his earnings.”

Decimus nodded. “I see.”

What a boring, pointless exchange, Camilla thought. Those kinds of conversations made up her life with Decimus. Surely, though, that was better than what Cornelia endured with Titus.

A new slave waited attentively near the doorway. Camilla wondered briefly what he thought of this greeting between man and wife who hadn't seen one another for almost ten months. But there wasn't much the slaves didn't know—or guess. This one would soon know all the surmises about master and mistress. The thought depressed her, made her feel exposed and vulnerable, all her saddest secrets fodder for gossip in the kitchen and hallways and stables.

“Why so somber, Camilla?”

“Somber, Decimus? Not at all,” she said briskly. “In fact, I have exciting news. Terentia will be married in a few weeks and Papa is planning a wonderful wedding.”

“Really! I can't believe our little Terentia's grown to be a bride. Who's the fortunate fellow?”

Camilla described the groom-to-be, but she knew Decimus didn't really care. He listened politely. “Well,” he said finally, “that's very nice. I hope their marriage turns out as well as ours.”

Rage flamed through Camilla. How dare he? What a perverse and ugly and hateful remark. When she made no reply, he continued in his light, mocking voice, “Don't you agree, Camilla, that we have a very civilized arrangement?”

She gave a tiny shrug. "I haven't given it much thought."

He raised a dark eyebrow. "Really? I'd have wagered you'd thought about everything, Camilla." He looked past Camilla, through the open archway into the courtyard. "I say, Camilla, I saw most of the staff when I arrived, but where are Ajax and Alex?"

There was a long moment of silence.

Alex and Ajax, the faun-like Greek twins with smooth young bodies and wise eyes.

"They're all right, aren't they?" Decimus asked sharply.

"They're fine. The doctor had wonderful success with them, but I thought the sea air would still be better for them. They're at the villa."

Decimus relaxed. "They're very valuable, you know." He smiled, good-humored now. "Camilla, I don't think you share my enthusiasm for twins. One of nature's remarkable feats. I find them fascinating."

"I know you do."

"Ah, well, we'll send for them. I want them to meet my beauties." He turned and called out, "Priscus?"

Camilla looked around.

Priscus stood by the archway. "Yes, my lord."

"Bring the boys in. I want the mistress to meet them."

Water splashed in the central fountain, spewing cheerfully from a tilted vase held by a sculpted maenad. Birds twittered in a cage hung in one corner. Camilla stood stiffly in the midst of splendor. She knew what was coming and dreaded it.

The boys came slowly into the hall. They were even younger than Alex and Ajax, twelve years old at the most. Instead of soft, dark skin, they were so fair they looked like wraiths in the soft light of the reception hall. Long blond hair hung in soft wisps around their delicate faces, emphasizing the startling blue of their eyes. They came in slowly, fearfully, darting shy, uncertain glances at Decimus, then at her.

Mixed with her recoil was a stabbing sense of shame and sorrow—and pity.

"Where did you get them?" she asked, her throat dry.

"My dear, it was an incredible piece of luck. I just happened to stop in at the slave market in Alexandria on the way home. Of course, you hear there are all kinds of wonders available there. At a price. The boys were just off a boat from Britain. I think they're German. Beautiful, aren't they?"

Camilla swallowed. "They're very young, Decimus."

He nodded. "Very young," he repeated softly. His tone sickened her. He knew how she felt, of course. His quick little smile, a wry twist of those sensuous lips, told her that.

It wasn't until that moment that she remembered quite how much she hated him, not until he stood there, with his narrow, clever face, and she heard again his light mocking voice and saw the hot lusting light in his eyes as he looked at his new boys.

This was her husband, this dark stranger who loved little boys.

"Priscus can show the boys to their quarters," Camilla said coldly. "You will want to rest after your long journey, Decimus." She turned to go.

"Wait, Camilla. Don't fly away when I've just got home. I would like to talk with you for a little while." He looked at Priscus. "Take the boys to my room. I'll be there shortly."

So now there was to be no subterfuge at all. She'd known the truth, of course, for a long time, since soon after their marriage. At first, she'd known only, with a feeling of diminishment, that Decimus wasn't interested in her, that he kept the Greek twins near him at night. Slowly, insidiously, she'd realized his relationship with the children wasn't that of master and slaves. Always, her mind shied away from explicit description. She would block out of her mind the soft little sounds the twins made at dinner as they sat beside Decimus and he reached out to caress them.

Priscus and the new young slaves walked away.

Decimus turned to Camilla with a worried frown. "Camilla, I want you to have a dinner party."

She looked at him searchingly. What could possibly make a dinner party important enough to discuss on his first morning home?

"I want you to invite Titus and Cornelia."

Camilla had always avoided inviting her sister and brother-in-law because she didn't like Titus, she never had.

"Why?"

"I need a friend at the Palace."

Camilla thought of his last letter with its hints of enemies and troubles to come. This desperate emphasis on a dinner party to reinforce himself with friends in high places meant he must indeed be in serious trouble.

"What have you done?" she asked baldly.

"Nothing wrong," he retorted sharply. "I've served the Empire well. There are always those who are jealous. I don't think anything will come of it, but I intend to take precautions."

"I see." She paused. "I don't like to invite my sister on that basis."

"You'll invite her," Decimus said quietly.

There was no mistaking the tone of threat.

"Why will I do that?" she demanded.

"To please me." Again, he gave that quick little smile that infuriated her. "Besides, it will keep peace in your family. I heard some very interesting gossip when I stopped at the Galbuses's villa on my way home."

Camilla knew Antonio and Tullia Galbus very well indeed. She knew their quick and darting wit and absolute delight in malicious rumors.

"We had a very interesting visit," Decimus continued silkily. "I understand Cornelia truly enjoys sporting events. In fact, they say she's made some close friends—some very intimate friends—among the charioteers and even with a gladiator, one whose family disowned him a few years ago. I believe he's known as Scorpus the Great even though he's really part of the Claudius family."

"You can't believe a word the Galbuses say," Camilla said flatly.

"They know everyone. What they say is awful, but usually it's right. Of course, I'd hate to have to tell your father what I heard."

"Decimus, you can't tell him."

He spread his hands gracefully. "My dear, I wouldn't dream of it." He smiled. "Now, about the dinner party . . ."

Slowly, Camilla nodded. "All right, Decimus, I'll have your dinner party." She paused, said, "I'll plan a very special party."

"You'll invite Titus and Cornelia." He wanted it understood.

She nodded. "Yes, and I think Papa and Terentia. That will leave us three places. Is there anyone else you'd like to ask?"

Decimus frowned thoughtfully, then said decisively, "Yes, put Quintus Calvus on the list."

Camilla remembered him, a pudgy banker.

"And maybe Spurious Lucullus," Decimus added.

"That sounds good," Camilla agreed. "Now, let me see." She frowned, but she knew what she was going to do. She'd made up her mind. In the space of this half-hour reunion with Decimus, she'd been angered, sickened, and blackmailed. So she knew what she was going to do. She looked up at Decimus with a bland expression, "I've an idea. We have a new neighbor near our villa at Neapolis. A friend told me he's now in Rome."

"A new neighbor?"

"Yes, old Senator Paulus's son, Marcus. He's just back from

several years in Greece. They say he's going to be a wonderful advocate."

"Marcus Paulus," Decimus repeated musingly. "Isn't that the name of the fellow who saved you?"

She looked at him sharply.

"From your tumble off the cliff," Decimus continued. "Of course, we must invite him. I owe him a great debt for having saved my delightful wife. By all means, Camilla."

Content now with his victory over the dinner party, Decimus chatted for a moment longer about the arrangements, then excused himself on the plea of freshening up after his journey.

Camilla stood in the reception hall and stared after him. So he urged her by all means to invite Marcus. He knew all about her rescue. From Priscus, of course.

Perhaps she was a fool to invite Marcus. If she invited him and if . . . oh, all the uncertainty and longing in her heart was bound up in that little word . . . if she and Marcus fell in love and Decimus ever learned of it, he would have the most potent weapon in the world to control her.

Camilla shook her head. There was no certainty Marcus would accept her invitation or, should he accept it, no certainty he would be willing to become her lover.

Marcus wanted a wife.

She could give him her love, but not her life.

Camilla whirled around and walked out into the courtyard. Did she dare send the invitation? If she dared, would Marcus come? If he came, what would happen then? Camilla paused beside the farthest fountain and stared at the golden image of Adonis, glistening in the sunlight, glorious and bold, but not nearly as exciting as her memory of Marcus, the sunlight touching his naked body with flame as he arched high off the cliff and dived down, down, down into a deep dark pool.

The two days before the party flew by. Camilla planned the menu and instructed Phoebe to be certain her yellow gown, the newest one, was back from the cleaners.

The evening of the dinner, Phoebe fluttered excitedly. "Miss Camilla, you look so lovely. I've never seen your eyes so bright."

The hairdresser gave a final twist to the soft curls that framed Camilla's face. "Your hair is perfect now."

Camilla held the circular silver mirror and stared at her soft reflection. Lustrous pearl earrings and a necklace of matched pearls gleamed.

Camilla felt a wave of faintness as she stared at her ghostly image. Did her face reveal her? Would others guess tonight that for the first time in her life she was consciously and deliberately looking beyond the boundaries she'd always accepted?

Would Marcus come?

A hand dropped on her shoulder. Camilla gasped.

"My dear, I didn't mean to startle you," Decimus said. "It's time to go meet our guests."

After a tiny instant of hesitation, Camilla rose and slipped her arm through his.

When they reached the steps, Decimus paused and said, "D'you know, Camilla, I don't believe I've ever seen you look lovelier."

A harpist sat in a shadowy corner of the reception hall. She plucked the strings gently and the soft, golden music flowed like water slipping over mountain rocks. Camilla smiled and talked to Quintus Calvus, then excused herself with a smile when the doorkeeper announced her father's arrival.

"Papa, I'm so happy you and Terentia could come tonight."

"We're honored by your invitation," he said gravely. He turned and embraced Decimus. "It's good to have you home. We're eager to hear of your good works in Syria."

Decimus looked at the older man sharply, then said slowly, "I had a challenging time out there, Senator, but nothing too remarkable happened. I understand we're going to have a celebration here soon," and he smiled at Terentia.

Camilla looked at her youngest sister with her round, open face and childish body. She was very young.

Terentia flushed happily. "Only a few weeks now, Decimus. You are coming, aren't you?"

Decimus slipped his arm around Terentia's shoulders. "I wouldn't miss it for the world."

Camilla's face tightened. Then she realized her younger sister was looking at her in dismay and she forced a smile. Terentia beamed in return.

The doorkeeper announced Titus and Cornelia. Decimus immediately moved forward to greet them and Senator Scipio looked at Camilla in surprise. Camilla whispered to her father, "I talked to Cornelia last week, Papa."

Suddenly, he looked worn and worried.

Camilla touched his arm. "It's all right, Papa. She's still Cornelia, the Cornelia we love."

The relief in her father's face shook her, but, when he turned to greet Cornelia and drew her into a warm embrace, Camilla was glad she'd done it. Cornelia was the sister and daughter they'd always loved, elegant and regal, gentle and kind and loving. Whatever else she was didn't matter beside that.

But Camilla must warn Cornelia to be more discreet.

Decimus drew Quintus Calvus and Titus into a tight circle and set out to be charming, regaling them with one flattering anecdote after another.

The laughter was booming when Spurious Capito arrived. He held out his hands to Camilla. "I'm glad Decimus is home again if that's what it takes to be able to see you."

Camilla smiled. "Spurious, you're very appealing to women. I'm surprised you're still single."

"My dear, if I succumbed to wedded bliss, I couldn't admire all the lovely ladies in Rome. As it is, I'm free to gain pleasure where I can."

Decimus clapped a hand on his shoulder. "That kind of talk could get you in trouble, Spurious, but you're all bark and no bite."

"A sly dog doesn't reveal his intentions."

Camilla continued the badinage, but gracefully avoided Spurious's embrace, and all the while she was listening to hear the front door open again.

Was Marcus coming?

Decimus clapped his hands. "I doubt there's a gayer group in Rome tonight. Now that we're all here, we'll have dinner."

"Decimus, we still lack a guest."

Decimus shrugged. "Perhaps he isn't coming. But he can join us at the table."

"My lord, my lady, Marcus Julius Paulus," the doorkeeper announced.

Everyone turned toward the entryway.

Camilla's first thought was how imposing he looked in a toga, how his presence diminished the other men.

Marcus nodded gravely. "Good evening, Senator Scipio and Camilla."

Her father moved forward eagerly to take his hand and introduce him to Decimus. Camilla didn't listen to the story of her rescue. Instead, she looked at Marcus and he at her and it was almost as if the two of them were alone together. Camilla felt a pang of fear. Surely everyone could tell! Surely they could sense the excitement and longing and desire linking her to Marcus. Her eyes cut nervously around the room. Everyone looked as usual, Decimus sly as if secretly amused, Titus overpoweringly vigorous, her father gravely severe. Then Decimus was shepherding everyone down the steps and into the courtyard along the central mosaic path to the dining room at the far end of the colonnade. Camilla walked beside Decimus, but she was intensely aware of Marcus, following behind her.

When they reached the dining room, all of the men except her father shed their heavy togas to reveal the newly fashionable light tunics popular for dining. The diners took their places, she and Decimus and her father on the center couch to their right and the other three men, including Marcus, to their left. Slaves washed their hands then quickly knelt to remove their shoes and wash their feet. A faint scent of rose water hung in the air. The slaves spread napkins in front of the diners who reclined on their left elbows across the couches, facing the table.

Courses followed one after another, hors d'oeuvres of oysters, olives, and lettuce, a main course featuring roasted kid and baked sole, fresh asparagus, truffles and mushrooms. The slaves constantly replenished the small silver wine cups with fine Sorrentine wine mixed with water.

Decimus turned to Marcus. "I understand you're going to be a second Cicero."

"That would be any advocate's dream," Marcus replied.

Quintus boomed, "I say, young man, I've heard of you. Didn't you handle a case in old Sabrinas's court yesterday?

Marcus nodded.

Quintus looked at him with respect. "They say you made one of the finest orations heard in Rome in years. I heard about it at the baths. You got the man off and everybody'd said it couldn't be done."

Decimus's heavy-lidded eyes narrowed. "Was that you, Marcus?"

"Yes."

Quintus took another deep draught of wine. "Wish I'd been there. It's the talk of the town."

"One case doesn't make a career," Marcus replied.

"It's a good beginning," Senator Scipio said firmly.

"Speaking of court cases," Decimus began, "did you hear . . ." He told an outrageous story of a will forgery case that had everyone laughing. He dominated the rest of the conversation except that in every way he flattered and deferred to Titus and Quintus.

Camilla smiled pleasantly and talked to her younger sister and thought, with a growing disdain, how grateful she was that she didn't love Decimus. It would be shaming to care for someone who obviously and deliberately exploited his guests' conceits. Titus and Quintus blossomed under the attention.

Camilla looked covertly at her father. Didn't he notice? Didn't he sense the desperate undercurrent to Decimus's gaiety? But her father was deep in conversation with Cornelia, his eyes shining with happiness.

Cornelia, too, looked happy, until midway through the meal when a wine-sodden Titus reached out to toy with a ringlet of his wife's hair. Camilla knew instantly the revulsion that flowed through Cornelia, but her older sister continued to lay quietly on the couch, making no move to escape that heavy hand. Camilla saw, too, that Titus knew his wife hated his touch. His loose mouth spread in a little wider smile, and Camilla knew she was seeing calculated cruelty.

Occasionally, Camilla responded to Spurious's continuing banter, but she felt as if the conversation, the deepness of the men's voices, the light tones of the women, the soft plucking of the harp, the hurried slap of the slaves' feet on the pavement, all combined to mask deep eddies of feeling that swirled beneath the social surface—Decimus's frantic effort to ingratiate, her father's relieved absorption in his eldest daughter, the hatred that quivered between Cornelia and Titus, and, to her, stronger than any of them, shouting to be discovered, the current of feeling between her and Marcus.

Marcus lay just to her left, only a foot away. Once their hands touched as they both reached for an apple for dessert.

Camilla drew her breath in sharply.

Marcus stared at her, his face somber.

Was he angry?

She didn't know. But he had come tonight.

Camilla wrenched her gaze away. She must be careful, but a sidelong glance at Decimus reassured her. He was too bound up in his conversation with Titus to notice her or Marcus.

When dessert ended, Decimus invited Titus to order the next round of drinks. Camilla's father frowned. He disliked drinking bouts, and Titus was already flushed and boisterous.

Camilla raised her voice above Titus's laughter. "I've arranged a concert in the courtyard for those who would enjoy some music."

Her father waved for his sandals. "Terentia and I would like that. Cornelia, will you join us?"

The party divided, Decimus remaining in the quickly-freshened dining room with Titus, Quintus, and Spurious. As Camilla led the way to the clump of wicker furniture near the central fountain, she heard Decimus call out, "How about a game, my lads?" Soon, the dice would click and excited shouts rise on the warm evening air.

Cushioned couches sat on either side of the fountain. Terentia and Cornelia took the first couch along with their father. After a moment's hesitation, Camilla and Marcus walked past them and the fountain and reclined on the other couch, a line of scarlet cushions between them.

The harpist began to play and rising waves of golden-light music rippled like softly warm water.

The water of the fountain cascaded like a silver curtain, effectively screening Camilla and Marcus from the view of her father and sisters.

Marcus looked at her intently. "Why did you ask me here tonight, Camilla?"

She stared down at the intricate embroidery on a red silk cushion.

"Is it just to torture me?" he demanded, his voice low and strained.

"No. I wanted to be near you." Slowly she met his searching gaze.

"Seeing you with him is torture," he continued huskily. "To know that you and he—" His words broke off.

"He and I what?" Camilla asked.

"He's your husband," Marcus said through clenched teeth. "He's home after almost a year's absence. I picture him touching you. It makes me sick."

Camilla looked nervously to her left, but the shining spray of water made this moment as private as any in a lover's bower. She turned toward Marcus. "I want to tell you something," she said gravely.

His dark, strong face was only inches from her own.

Camilla clasped her hands tightly together. "It is the story of a girl and her marriage," she continued.

"I don't want to hear." His voice was rough.

"Please, Marcus, listen to me," she insisted, her voice light as the sweep of a bird's wing. "When this girl married, she was frightened. She didn't know what to expect, but there are whispers among girls and laughter at the baths. There is a sense of mystery and excitement. Girls know this will be resolved on their wedding night. On my wedding night, I lay on the wedding couch and waited . . ."

Marcus began to push up from the couch. Camilla reached out and held his arm, feeling bold, yet calm at the same time.

". . . and waited. Finally, I fell asleep, using my wedding veil to wipe away the tears."

The muscles in his jaw bunched. "Do you think I want to know what happened?"

She interrupted, "Don't you understand? Nothing happened."

"Nothing?" He sank back onto the couch and stared at her. Slowly, very slowly, like sunlight edging above the horizon at dawn, his face softened. "Camilla, do you mean Decimus didn't make love to you?"

She nodded. "I thought perhaps it was my fault, that he found me ugly, repulsive. I grieved. I admit that, but now I'm so grateful. I should die if he ever touched me."

"He's crazy," Marcus whispered loudly, laughter and happiness bubbling in his voice.

"Shh," Camilla warned.

Marcus reached out and grabbed her hand and held it hard. Delight brimmed in his dark eyes. "Camilla, tell me again. He's never touched you." He paused and asked again, "Never? Not on any night?"

"Never."

"I'd like to shout," he exulted. "I'd like to stand up and throw benches in the air and race and yell. If you knew the kinds of things I've imagined . . ."

She blushed at that, her eyes falling away from his, but the desire she glimpsed there excited her, made her feel breathless and terribly alive and young and lovely.

The golden chords of the harp swept to a crescendo, dropped delicately away. The harpist looked inquiringly at Camilla, but before she could call for more she heard the others rising from the wicker couch on the other side of the shimmering wall of water. Quickly, Camilla pulled her hand free from Marcus and they, too, rose. They stood decorously apart, hostess and guest. She turned to face her father. "Must you go so soon, Papa?"

He glanced up at the darkening sky, brilliantly streaked with crimson and mauve and purest gold. "It's getting dark, Camilla. Terentia and I'd better be on our way. I don't know when I've enjoyed an evening as much." He reached out and drew her close. "A very special evening," he murmured.

He looked up at Marcus. "Delighted to know your case went so well. We're going to hear great things from you, young man."

"I'll do my best, sir."

Senator Scipio turned to a waiting slave. "Call our litters." Then he asked Cornelia, "Are you going home now or will you wait for Titus?"

Cornelia glanced at Camilla and Marcus, said casually, "I believe I'll go home now, Papa. Titus knows the way. He'll be very late."

Raucous laughter burst from the dining room.

Cornelia knows, Camilla thought suddenly, and she's going home so Marcus and I can be alone. My dear sister, Camilla thought, my very dear sister.

Camilla embraced Cornelia. "I'll talk to you soon."

Marcus and Camilla stayed by the fountain as the others moved away. When they were gone, Camilla faced Marcus and the look in his eyes made her heart beat faster.

"Would you like to walk in the park?" she asked.

"Yes."

They walked carefully, not touching, but Camilla had never in her life been so aware of a man's nearness. At the gate, she hesitated, "We mustn't be gone long."

Marcus reached out and took her hand and the warmth and strength of his grasp ignited a spark that Camilla knew could easily erupt into flame.

Hand in hand, they walked swiftly up the graveled path as it wound between tall, thin fir trees in a dim and private tunnel. At its end, they stepped into a dusky arbor heavy with honeysuckle. With no words now, with an urgency born of desire, the first flickering tongues of that flame, they moved into each other's arms and Marcus's mouth closed over hers, demanding, exciting, promising. The he buried his face against her neck. "Camilla, Camilla, Camilla," he murmured. "You're going to be mine. All mine. No one else's."

"Marcus," she whispered.

His lips moved against her cheek, seeking her mouth. "Hmm?"

"Marcus, we must think."

But once again, his mouth found hers and there was no time for thought, only for feeling. She gloried in the softness and warmth of his lips touching hers. Finally, reluctantly, her voice soft and hurried, she repeated, "Marcus, we must think."

He laughed. "I don't need to think. I know all that matters. I'm going to have you and no one else."

Her hands pressed against his back. Dear Marcus. Beloved Marcus. "But you must think," she insisted. "You want a wife. I can't be your wife. I asked you to come tonight so I could tell you I love you, but you don't have to promise me anything."

Once again, his mouth possessed hers. Camilla felt swept to a dizzying height, and for the first time in her life, she was near to losing all control. Her breath began to come in quick, sharp gasps.

Again, he laughed, a full, rich laugh of delight and joy. "Camilla, I'm going to love you until—"

Gravel crackled underfoot.

They stiffened and jerked apart.

Hastily, Camilla straightened the folds of her gown, turned to look out of the arbor.

"Mistress?"

"It's Priscus," Camilla said.

"Tell him to be damned," Marcus growled.

"I can't. I don't dare. Marcus, I hate this. I want to love you, but to have to sneak and hide is dreadful. I hate it."

"We won't hide." Marcus stepped to the arbor entrance. "Hello there," he called out.

"Oh, is it you, Sir?" Priscus peered through the gloom. "I came to see if the mistress needed a torch."

Camilla stepped beside Marcus. "How thoughtful of you, but we can still see. We'll be in shortly. You may return to the house, Priscus."

He bowed and turned and began the long walk down the curving path between the fir trees.

When he was out of view, Camilla said, "I'm sorry, Marcus."

He reached out and pulled her near. "Hush, Camilla. It's all right. You and I are going to be together. Somehow." He held her tightly. "Come and meet me tomorrow. At Aristides's ivory shop on the Via Lata."

She stared at him with wide, imploring eyes.

"Don't be frightened," he said gently. "Come and meet me. Tomorrow."

IX

A bird trilled sweetly in the first gray light of dawn. Camilla flung back her cover and slipped into her sandals. She pulled open the shutters and saw the beginnings of daylight.

Today.

She hugged herself and shivered.

Today.

Oh Papa, I love him so much, she thought. You would be distraught if you knew, but love comes only once and I must reach out with both hands and take what happiness I may.

Today.

The slave girl, Antonia, straggled sleepily into the room. "Mistress, do you wish to dress?"

"My gray stola, Antonia. I'm going to take a walk."

Antonia rubbed her eyes. "It's so early, Mistress. Don't you want your breakfast first?"

Camilla shook her head impatiently. "Not now. When I return."

Dew glistened on the marble statues and the shrubs in the courtyard. A few leaves drifted in the fountain pools. Camilla hurried through the courtyard and pushed through the gate. She followed the path she and Marcus had taken the night before.

Birds chattered cheerfully and their gay little song echoed the happy refrain in Camilla's heart: today, today, today.

The park behind the house sloped uphill. Camilla passed the arbor and climbed a steep path to a summerhouse that overlooked the city below. She leaned against the wooden railing and stared out at the magnificence of Rome at first light. On the hill opposite spread the overpowering Palace of Caligula. She turned and looked down into the city, glimpsing the Forum. Already, streets were filling as toga-clad men hurried to early morning audiences with those superior to them in rank and wealth. The senators and knights, of course, brushed through the crowds to visit the Emperor.

Camilla breathed deeply of the fresh, cool air. Down below, the crowded streets would be choked with dust and smoke from restaurant and bakery fires. She stayed in the summerhouse until the cool edge of morning gave way to midmorning heat. She wanted to be certain Decimus was gone before she went back to the house.

She didn't want to see Decimus today. Especially not today.

Camilla glanced down at her wedding ring. She turned it slowly on her finger. The golden band shone brilliantly. The ring was meaningless, signified nothing. She felt not a twinge of guilt or regret. She wasn't going to take anything from Decimus, because he'd never wanted her. She was his wife in name only.

Her father didn't know that.

Camilla bit her lip. Wouldn't even her father recognize that love has a claim on the heart? Decisively, she shook her head. She wasn't going to think of either Decimus or her father today. Today belonged to Marcus.

She smiled, recalling Marcus, remembering everything about him—the way he stood, the look in his eyes, the feel of his hand, the pressure of his mouth on hers.

As she walked slowly back down the path, she thought of Marcus, of his smile and the way it curved his mouth, of his eyes and their dark intensity, of the breadth of his chest and the strength in his legs. She felt swept by glory, enveloped by love.

Marcus loved her. She knew that was true in her heart, knew it as surely as the beat of her own. Marcus loved her and she loved Marcus, and today she was going to know the truth of love.

Was love as glorious as the poets said?

Phoebe was waiting anxiously by the courtyard gate. When she saw Camilla, she hurried forward. "Camilla, you've been gone so long and Anna said you went without a bite of breakfast."

"I don't need food today," Camilla replied.

"But you must eat. You'll be faint by lunch."

Camilla shook her head impatiently. "I'm going to bathe and then I'm going down to town."

"Bathe? Here at the house?"

They did, of course, have their own bathing rooms as did most of the very rich, but to bathe in the morning was strange indeed.

Camilla nodded firmly. "Yes. I want rose water and perfumed oil. Call Galla. I want my hair done."

Phoebe scurried ahead. Camilla waited a while, listening to the trill of birds until the bath was ready. When she was fresh and pink and lightly toweled by Phoebe, she slipped into a fresh tunic and sat on a stool while Galla combed her hair.

"Put silver clips here and here," Camilla directed.

Galla chattered happily, but Phoebe watched with a puzzled frown.

When Camilla bent forward to study her jewel case, Phoebe asked, "Where are you going, Camilla?"

Camilla lifted out a necklace of delicate silver whorls inset with gleaming opals. "I'm going to do some shopping," she answered carelessly. "I may drop by Cornelia's. Or perhaps I'll go to the baths. I haven't decided." Camilla shrugged away Phoebe's concern, though obviously Phoebe suspected something was afoot. But Phoebe was loyal to her, the only person in the home she could trust absolutely.

Camilla thought of that again when she was climbing into her litter and overheard Priscus asking Phoebe her destination. Phoebe said quickly, "Oh, she and Lady Cornelia are meeting. Probably it's something to do with the wedding."

Dear Phoebe.

Camilla leaned back in her litter. She left open the curtains. Rome baked this September afternoon. The canopy of the litter held her in a pocket of heat, but a smile touched her lips.

Today, her heart sang, today.

The litter slanted sharply downward as her bearers scrambled down the steep roadway. Traffic thickened as they neared the base of the hill. Pedestrians elbowed and shoved. When they passed the Temple of Diana, Camilla smiled at a fuzzy little monkey on a leash doing tricks for coins. Her bearers struggled against a swarm of peddlers and rabble on their way to the Coliseum. A troupe of elephants trumpeted excitedly, their keepers jabbing them with sharp hooks to keep them to the center of the narrow street. They, too, would be on their way to the Coliseum. Camilla looked at their leathery skins and dark-brown eyes with long feathery lashes and felt a wave of compassion. How horrid it was to know that these huge animals would soon be teased with flames into madness then turned loose to battle criminals as thousands and thousands of idlers screamed themselves hoarse in delight. Even now, she faintly heard a wash of voices rising, rising. She covered her ears, for roars meant death, and she hated to think of death on a sunny day before love.

Her train wound its way along the Tiber. Turgid yellow water glistened like oily gold in the late morning heat. Not far ahead, she saw the gleaming facades of the huge baths and shopping areas of the Campus Martius. Camilla motioned to the leader of her bearers, who trotted alongside in bright red livery. "Felix, I wish to go first to the shop of the Greek jeweler two doors down from the entrance to the baths."

The jeweler's daughter welcomed Camilla into the shop. Light streamed through slitted windows onto tables holding cushions covered with sparkling rings and bracelets and necklaces.

The proprietor bustled up. "My lady, can I show you some pearls today? They've just arrived from Alexandria and they are the loveliest I've ever seen, fit only for a woman of your rank."

"Not today. But there is something I'd like you to do for me." Camilla explained what she wanted.

The proprietor frowned. "I don't know, my lady, but we will try. Yes, indeed, we will certainly try." He clapped his hands. A grizzled artisan hobbled into the front of the shop. He, too, listened to Camilla's request.

The proprietor brought a stool. Camilla sat down. The artisan studied her profile for a long moment, began to sketch on a sheet of papyrus. When he was finished, he spoke to the shop owner in Greek, then disappeared into the back of the shop. It wasn't long, not quite half an hour, when he returned with a small, thin piece of silver. He held it out to Camilla.

"It's perfect, just perfect." It was a silhouette of her face in profile and a very good likeness. "Put it in a silver locket."

She carried the locket in her hand as she returned to her litter. Her lead bearer waited for her instructions. Camilla didn't hesitate. "To the shop of Aristides on the Via Lata."

Today, Camilla thought wonderingly, as her litter jolted

swiftly ahead. She held tight to the little locket. Today, today. When the litter stopped in front of the ivory shop, Camilla felt her heart begin to race.

"Here is Aristides's shop, my lady," Felix said. He reached out to help her from the litter. When she stood on the pavement, Camilla felt so alone. She must cross the threshold or not, it was her decision. If her father ever knew, his heart would be broken. But what of her heart? Should love stay locked in darkness and wither like spring flowers deprived of sun and rain? Camilla looked over her shoulder. "I will be several hours, Felix." The bearer nodded. Camilla lifted her chin and walked into the dim shop.

Intricately carved ivory from Ceres glimmered in the dim light. A curtain moved at the back of the room. An old man shuffled toward her, smiling in welcome. "If you will come this way, my lady."

Camilla pushed through the bright green curtain. She stood alone in a dusty, narrow passageway. She heard footsteps, firm and quick, and Marcus hurried down the interior stairs. Even in the dim light, she could see his smile. He reached out to take her hands and hold them tightly.

"I feel your pulse. It beats as quickly as a frightened bird's." Marcus drew her close and bent down to gently kiss her throat.

"Oh, Marcus," she whispered.

"Don't be frightened, my love. Don't ever be frightened with me."

He slipped an arm around her shoulders and they walked up the dusty stone steps. Marcus opened the heavy wooden door at the landing and they stepped into a magnificent apartment with delicate pastel frescoes in the reception hall. It was a long apartment of dim and quiet rooms, cool and secluded, far from the street noises and the boisterous shouts from the nearby baths.

"Welcome to my home."

Camilla looked about. "It's very quiet."

Marcus nodded. "I've sent all the slaves away this afternoon. There's only you and I."

They looked into each other's eyes.

Alone together, Camilla thought. For lovers, there could be no happier moment.

Marcus slowly pulled Camilla to him. She came willingly. They stood together. Their mouths met and Camilla knew a rush of delight filled with a promise of feelings she'd never known. Her hands held his cheeks and his arms tightened about her and her body molded to his. They kissed with sweet, wild excitement, then, abruptly, he held her at arm's length, looking at her with joy and delight. "Camilla," he cried exuberantly, "you are the loveliest woman in the world, the most desirable. I'll never be able to tell you how I feel." He paused, said almost shyly, "I want to show you what I've made for you."

He tugged at her hand, eagerly leading her past a shallow center pool. Goldfish darted in the clear water, glistening like bursts of sunlight. He led her past the study and opened the door to a small sleeping chamber. A window in the wall opposite opened into the courtyard and light streamed inside. Marcus gestured almost diffidently to his left. Camilla turned. She looked at the wall and a rush of happiness swept her. The painting was only begun, but Camilla recognized the place with a sense of wonder. She turned toward Marcus, tears brimming in her eyes. He'd painted the rocky bluff above black rocks and surging, thirsting blue water. Standing on the bluff was a woman, her dress molded against her by the whipping wind.

"Now you'll always be near me," Marcus said softly. He held out his arms and she stepped into them, realizing as she did how right and good it felt to embrace Marcus. She nuzzled her face against his neck, lifted her head to smile at him. "I brought you a gift." She pulled the locket from her dress and handed it to him.

He opened the locket, smiled, and raised it to his lips.

She said quietly, almost gravely. "I've never been this happy in all my life."

His answer was equally grave. "That's what I want for you, Camilla. I want you always to be happy."

They looked into each other's eyes for a long moment. Camilla took a quick breath and loosed her gown. The look in Marcus's eyes reminded her of a night when a glorious shower of meteors streaked across the western sky. The dress sank in folds beneath her feet. Camilla stepped out of the mound of soft wool and, quickly, slipped free of her tunic and undergarments.

Swiftly, Marcus removed his toga and pulled off his tunic. They faced each other, their limbs slim and clear in the soft light of the afternoon. They moved together into each other's arms, their mouths joining hungrily, moving and touching and feeling. Passion swept them as waters tumble over a cataract, faster and faster and faster. They murmured to each other and moved as in a dream toward his bed and sank down together. She loved the feel of his body, its warmth and pressure and strength. His hands loved her, touching so lightly her breasts and the inside of her thighs. Warmth and desire spread through her until she was straining to pull him closer and suddenly the glory of streaking meteors couldn't compare with the explosive joy of their union.

When they lay quietly, Marcus's hand gently twined her thick dark hair. Camilla smiled sleepily into his eyes. "I love you."

He kissed the tip of her nose. "I love you."

"I wish . . ."

Marcus raised up on an elbow to look down into her face. "What do you wish?"

She reached up and spread her hand against his chest. "I wish we could stay here forever."

"Camilla, let me talk to your father."

She drew her breath in sharply. "Marcus, promise me you won't. I know what Papa would do. He would have me banished. I know he would." She shivered though the afternoon heat lay thick and heavy as a sheepskin in the small room.

"Don't be frightened, Camilla. I won't do anything to cause you trouble."

Tears trembled in her eyes. "I shouldn't have come. I shouldn't have loved you because it can lead to nothing and you deserve a woman who can be your wife. I should never have come."

His mouth closed onto hers, violently, fiercely. He kissed her for a long moment until she began to kiss him in return. His jaw hard against her cheek, he said suddenly, "Don't ever say that, Camilla. We belong together."

September was never lovelier in Rome. Camilla and Marcus met in Caesar's Gardens near the Tiber and walked hand in hand along unfrequented paths. They met at the Theater of Pompey to see the latest comedies. They met at the library near the gigantic statue of Augustus. Every afternoon, they came to Marcus's apartment. Some afternoons, they made love quickly. Some afternoons, they made love very slowly. Some afternoons they spoke of thoughts they'd never shared with others and quietly delighted in companionship.

One afternoon as the shadows began to lengthen and she knew she must soon go, Camilla nuzzled her face against his chest. "I can never have enough of you," she said huskily. She began to kiss his shoulder. Slowly, she moved her mouth, her lips a whispering caress, across his chest and into his hard flat stomach. Her hand brushed up his leg and spread to touch the muscles of his thigh.

"Camilla," he cried.

She laughed, a soft laugh of delight, as she aroused him and then there was no time for laughter and scarcely for breath, no time even to kiss, as desire exploded and they melded together.

When they lay quietly, their eyes tender, Camilla said regretfully, "I can't come tomorrow."

He frowned. "Why?"

"I'm going to Papa's house to get everything ready for the wedding." She reached out to touch his cheek. "I'll miss you."

"I'll miss you. A day without you will be like a prison sentence."

"You can get some work done."

"I have been working. I've handled five cases already this month."

"But never in the afternoon."

"Never, never, never in the afternoon," he agreed quickly.

Camilla didn't respond to the joyous tone in his voice. Instead, she looked at the almost finished fresco on the opposite wall. Her face was sad and pensive.

"Camilla, you look worried." His eyes were filled with concern.

She faced him, trying to understand the uneasiness that had been worming into her mind the last few days, awake or asleep. "I don't know if it's an omen, but I feel something is wrong." She shook her head in vexation. "These past weeks have been perfect, the happiest weeks I've ever spent. I have a dreadful feeling that it can't last, that something terrible is going to happen."

"Don't be fearful."

"Nothing perfect ever lasts," she said sadly. "Lovely flowers wither. A happy afternoon passes and can never be recaptured. Marcus, our time together has been too good, too wonderful."

"Nonsense," he said briskly. "This is what life's supposed to be like, Camilla. We know the secret, you and I."

"We can't steal off together every afternoon forever," she said quietly.

His silence told her that he, too, realized these dreamlike days could not be counted on. He reached for her hand and held it tightly, and she realized Marcus, too, was afraid.

After they dressed and were walking toward the door, he suddenly stopped and pulled her roughly into his arms. He pressed his face against her hair. "Promise me you're mine. For always."

"I promise." She hugged him and looked up, forcing a smile. "Don't worry," and now she was reassuring him. "Everything's going to be all right." They stared deeply into each other's eyes, both of them willing life to let them love.

"You'll be at the wedding, won't you?" Camilla asked brightly.

"Of course. I'll always come where you are."

She carried the memory of his face, intense and loving, as her litter jolted its way through the crowded streets. She arrived home just as Decimus was dismounting from his litter. He came and reached out his hand to help her step onto the pavement.

"I scarcely seem to see you anymore," Decimus observed.

Camilla looked at him sharply, but his face seemed just as usual, his dark eyes sardonic, his sensual mouth curved in a tiny smile.

"Oh," she said vaguely, "there's much to do for the wedding."

"Is Terentia excited?"

"Aren't all brides?" Camilla asked.

"But you've been there today?" Decimus persisted.

"No, I've been shopping today." She gestured toward her litter. "Some new perfumes. I'm going to Papa's house tomorrow. The wedding is the next day."

They talked about the wedding as they walked into the house, but Camilla wondered if Decimus was suspicious? Really, though, what difference would it make? He wouldn't divorce her and lose her dowry.

At dinner, they talked inconsequentially about the wedding and a business project that interested Decimus. He told her a story making the rounds of the Capitol, that Caligula had decided to make his horse, Incitatus, a consul because he felt certain Incitatus had as much sense as any Senator he knew.

She looked at him unsmiling. "That's not really true, is it?"

Decimus laughed uproariously. "Titus swears he heard him say it to old Senator Blandus. You know him. He's such a pompous ass."

Camilla shook her head. "Caligula shouldn't make fun of the Senators. They will be very angry."

Decimus shrugged. "Why should Caligula care? He loves to rile the old bores."

Camilla knew her father would be outraged. She wondered what Rome was coming to when its Emperor would make such a joke. She excused herself soon after dinner to go to bed. But, of course, that was the pattern of her life with Decimus. Her early departure wouldn't surprise him. As she lay in her darkened room with the latticed windows open onto the courtyard, she heard him call out, "Come here, boys. Hurry."

Camilla shuddered and put a pillow over her ears. But now she had her own world to think about. She could close Decimus out of her mind and she no longer carried his image into her sleep. She welcomed dreams now because they reunited her with Marcus. She remembered the touch of him, the feel of his mouth and hands. A dream was almost as wonderful as being with him.

Someday would dreams be all she would have of Marcus?

That thought woke her. She watched the dusky light of dawn edge into her room and felt alone and lonely. But this was the day before Terentia's wedding. She couldn't lie abed, swept with forebodings.

Camilla clapped her hand and her little slave girl hurried to her side. She dressed quickly, but took time and care in choosing the dress she would wear at the wedding tomorrow. She chose a soft, pale blue gown because Marcus had once told her that he loved her in blue. "In blue, your eyes are the color of sapphires, Camilla."

She thought of Marcus all the way to the Aventine Hill and her father's mansion.

Her father greeted her with an embrace. "Can we get everything ready for tomorrow?" he boomed.

"Of course we can, Papa."

Cornelia arrived by the fourth hour. The three of them paced through the house, directing the slaves who scattered sawdust on the floors then swept with brooms of palm and twigs. The fresh smell mingled with the scent of evergreen boughs stacked by the doorway to be hung for decoration. Other slaves frantically polished the silver plate because the wedding would be followed by a magnificent feast.

In the afternoon, Camilla and Cornelia hung tiny colored ribbons, scarlet and yellow and blue and green, from the entrance doorway. Terentia watched, her eyes filled with happiness.

Camilla nodded in approval. "Everything's beginning to look wonderful."

"Let's put some more myrtle over the entry to the study," Cornelia suggested.

Terentia followed them about in a daze until Cornelia gave her a hug and said firmly, "You go and rest now, honey. Camilla and I will see to everything."

Terentia nodded wordlessly and hurried off to her room.

Cornelia looked after her. "Do you think he's really a nice boy, Camilla?"

"I hope so. But who knows?"

"Surely one of us will be fortunate," Cornelia said bitterly.

Camilla touched her sister's arm. "Here comes Papa."

At dinner, no one managed to eat very much. Finally, Terentia put down her spoon. "It's time now to try on my wedding dress."

Her older sisters smiled and followed Terentia to her room. When she was dressed in a fresh undertunic, Cornelia lifted up the gleaming white wool wedding dress and slipped it over Terentia's head. When the fine white wool hung in gentle folds on her feet, Terentia reached up and took off the golden locket she'd worn since babyhood. Carrying it in her hands, Terentia and her sisters walked solemnly through the house to the reception hall. A shrine dedicated to the household gods sat in an alcove there. Terentia and her family knelt before the shrine and dedicated the locket to the gods.

When Terentia rose and stood looking down at the locket with a tiny smile, it seemed to Camilla that her little sister already seemed older. She wasn't a little girl anymore. She'd taken her first step to adulthood.

Camilla remembered the night before her own wedding and her excitement as she'd placed her locket on the shrine. She'd thought then that the morrow would bring her love and knowledge of what it meant to be a woman.

But she hadn't known love until this September in Rome.

"Camilla, Camilla."

She looked up, startled.

Terentia was laughing. "I don't think you've heard a word I've said."

"I'm sorry, Terentia. I must have been dreaming."

"Remembering your own wedding," Terentia said softly.

Their father spoke up behind them. "I'm a happy man tonight.

Soon I'll have three daughters safely and well wed. There aren't many men in Rome who can make that boast."

"Don't make boasts, Father," Cornelia cut in sharply.

Senator Scipio frowned.

Camilla said hurriedly, "We must see Terentia off to bed now. The first guests will be here at dawn."

Their father nodded. "We want Terentia well-rested." He lightly touched his youngest daughter's cheek. "I'll leave you to the care of your sisters, Terentia."

In Terentia's room, Cornelia helped her youngest sister remove the wedding dress and hang it in a cupboard. Camilla gently laid with the dress the flame-colored veil that Terentia would also wear at her wedding.

Camilla looked lovingly at her little sister. Terentia was almost plain, really, still a bit gawky and awkward at fifteen, but tonight excitement colored her cheeks and brought a sparkle to her eyes.

Terentia held out her hands to her sisters. "Don't go yet. I can't possibly sleep."

Camilla and Cornelia smiled indulgently and sat on the edge of Terentia's bed.

"Doesn't it remind you," Cornelia asked, "of when we were little and they would put us to bed but we'd slip out of our rooms and get together?"

Camilla laughed. "You were always the leader, Cornelia."

"Cornelia, you'd dare anything," Terentia said admiringly.

"It seems long ago," Cornelia said slowly. "We were happy then."

"We're happy now," Terentia exclaimed.

There was an instant's pause, then Cornelia said gently, "We're happy to be here tonight with you, Terentia."

Terentia looked from one older sister to the other, then blurted out, "Cornelia, Camilla . . ."

They looked at her inquiringly.

"Tell me," Terentia said shyly, "what is love like?"

Cornelia's russet hair glimmered like bronze in the flickering light from a cluster of lamps hanging behind Terentia's bed. Her green eyes were in shadow.

Camilla looked at Cornelia anxiously. If Roman gossip was true, Cornelia could describe the act of love in infinite variety. But that, of course, wasn't what Terentia wanted to know. Terentia wanted to know what it was that made a bond between a man and a woman. She wanted to know if caring for another more than self could actually be. She wanted to know if life's highest dreams could really come true.

Cornelia reached out and took her youngest sister's hand. "Love . . ." Cornelia repeated slowly. "Love is . . . Oh Terentia, I don't know what love is." Cornelia dropped Terentia's hand and jumped up and ran from the room.

Terentia's shocked face looked suddenly young again, very young and vulnerable. She turned to Camilla, tears streaking her cheeks. "What have I said? I thought Cornelia loved Titus."

Camilla said helplessly, "It's hard sometimes to know how others feel."

Terentia looked at her imploringly. "You're happy, aren't you, Camilla?"

Camilla looked away. She couldn't lie, but she couldn't frighten and dismay her little sister on the night before her wedding.

"You're in love, Camilla, aren't you?"

Camilla thought of Marcus and her face softened. "Yes, Terentia," she said softly. "I know about love. Love is wanting to be near someone every moment of the day. Love is hearing a melody when someone speaks his name. Love is being held close. Terentia, love is wonderful."

Terentia brightened. "Camilla," she said shyly, "Sextus is very handsome. Do you think he'll love me?"

Camilla looked at her little sister's open face and trusting eyes. "Well," she said fiercely, "he'd just better." She reached out and hugged Terentia, then continued more lightly, "We've settled all the questions of life tonight, haven't we? Too much more and you'll never get to sleep. Let me tuck you in now, Terentia." She pulled the cover up over her sister and bent to kiss her cheek. "Sleep well, my sweet. Tomorrow will be a wonderful day."

She closed Terentia's door behind her and walked out beneath the portico. Bars of moonlight patched the walkway. The sweet scent of honeysuckle wafted on the night breeze.

"Camilla."

Camilla saw Cornelia sitting on a marble bench next to the central fountain. Camilla joined her.

"Did I upset Terentia?"

Camilla shook her head. "It's all right."

"Did you tell her about me?"

"Of course not."

Cornelia reached up and clung to Camilla's hand. "I don't know what I've done to deserve a sister like you. Papa's right. You're very wonderful, Camilla."

"Hush, now. You're my sister."

"No matter what?"

"No matter what."

They were quiet for a moment, then Cornelia said bitterly, "I know Papa wouldn't feel that way if he knew."

"If he knew everything, his heart would understand."

Cornelia's mouth twisted with bitterness. "He'd think I should open my veins. That would be the only honorable choice left."

Camilla drew her breath in sharply. "You mustn't ever think like that."

Cornelia pressed her hands against her face for a moment. When they dropped away, her expression was empty. She reached out, took Camilla's hand. "Don't be frightened. I'd never do it. I don't care about being honorable." She tossed her head, said defiantly, "I want to gain as much happiness from life as I can and I don't give a fig about what a Roman matron should or shouldn't be. And I have my sons. I love them so much."

"I know you do." Camilla's heart ached. Why shouldn't Cornelia know happiness, too? Why did this wonderful sister have to endure a wretched marriage just so she could be with her sons? "Life is horribly unfair," Camilla said somberly.

Cornelia's lips curved in a half smile. "That's true, but perhaps knowing that gives us the courage to wrest the best we can from life." She laughed, the throaty laugh Camilla had always admired. "Don't grieve for me, Camilla. I have my moments. Some very wonderful moments."

"They can't last very long," Camilla said slowly, and she was thinking of her long and lovely afternoons with Marcus.

"True," Cornelia said simply. "But at least I've known them." She stood up, squeezed Camilla's hand once more, then let go. "We'd better get to bed now. It's getting late. But I wanted to be sure I hadn't ruined Terentia's evening."

"Everything's fine," Camilla assured her.

Cornelia's life wasn't fine at all, Camilla thought wearily as she slipped into a fresh tunic and prepared for bed. Cornelia was becoming notorious in Rome. Their father couldn't help but hear more gossip and then he'd come back to Camilla.

As for herself, now she lay once again in her father's house, as she had so long ago, thinking of love. But the love she lived for wasn't her husband's. If her father ever learned about her and Marcus, he would feel that she too had dishonored the family.

Camilla moved restlessly on the bed. Sleep wouldn't come. The last night she'd slept in this bed, she too had just removed her golden locket and left it on the household shrine. She'd looked ahead to the wedding couch where she would lay the next night. A wedding couch . . . She saw Marcus in her mind and her lips called his name. She reached out her hands but the bed lay empty next to her.

X

Terentia's shining black hair hung in six separate locks, as custom decreed, each tied with gaily colored ribbons. Cornelia stood on tiptoe to fasten a wreath of flowers in her hair, verbena and sweet marjoram and myrtle and orange blossoms.

Camilla stood back, her hands on her hips, and smiled at her sister. "You're the prettiest bride I've ever seen."

Terentia's face shone with happiness. "Do I really look pretty?" She twisted her head to try and peer out into the courtyard. "Is Sextus here yet?"

"I hope not," Cornelia said briskly, "but we're almost done." She leaned forward and rearranged the folds of Terentia's white gown.

"Are we ready to tie the lover's knot?" Camilla asked, holding up a tasseled cord.

"In a moment." Cornelia tugged and pulled at the gown. "There. That's perfect. Now we can tie the cord."

Camilla slipped the cord around Terentia's waist and tied it in a knot of Hercules. Only the groom could untie it.

A slave girl ran excitedly into Terentia's room. "They're here, Miss. They're here." The groom and his family had arrived.

Cornelia and Camilla hurried in a last-minute flurry, Camilla draping the flame-colored veil over Terentia's head, Cornelia rearranging the gossamer veil until it fell in a smooth straight line.

It was time.

As the families gathered in the reception hall, Camilla scanned the surging group of guests, who were jockeying for the best position to see the ceremony. Decimus stood near the family masks, as befitted a son-in-law. Camilla nodded at him but he was too busy talking to a banker to see. Camilla looked past him, and there, yes, she'd know Marcus's powerful build anywhere, there, almost hidden from view, she glimpsed him. She didn't smile. She knew she mustn't smile or the world would be able to read a lover's heart. He saw her and they gazed at each other for a long moment until Camilla turned away as the ceremony began.

Her father's sister, Lollia, stood in the center of the reception hall with Terentia and Sextus. Lollia was an imposing woman, tall with a beaked nose like her brother's. She was admired for her rectitude. It augured well for a marriage to be conducted by a woman such as Lollia.

She reached out to take Terentia's hand. The guests hushed. Lollia took Sextus's hand. Slowly, with great dignity, Lollia placed Terentia's hand within Sextus's.

In a faint voice, Terentia said, "When and where you are, there am I also."

Sextus replied in clear, ringing accents, "When and where you are, there am I also."

His last word was drowned in cheers.

"Congratulations."

"May happiness be upon you both."

Flute players burst into a fanfare. Guests swirled around the new couple, embracing and congratulating them.

In the happy and boisterous crowd, no one noticed when Camilla and Marcus spoke softly by the steps to the courtyard.

"Meet me in the arbor by the last fountain. No one will miss us," Marcus said softly.

To slip away to see Marcus was dangerous and foolish. Camilla knew that was true. She also knew she must be near him, that she couldn't withstand his call. Still, she looked nervously around the reception hall. Everyone was laughing and talking so fast it sounded like a flock of birds settling for the evening. Camilla edged through the crowd, pausing occasionally to chat with old friends and somehow managing not to reveal her impatience, her hurry. Once down the steps and into the courtyard, she walked swiftly along the central path with only a fleeting glance behind her. Most of the guests still jammed the reception hall, so the courtyard stretched empty ahead of her. Marble statuary screened the arbor by the last fountain and the arbor itself drooped beneath its thick cover of honeysuckle. Camilla ducked into its dimness and Marcus caught her up in his arms. They kissed and the world receded. There was nothing but the moment and the feel of Marcus's mouth and the pounding of her blood and the touch of his body against hers. Finally, swept by passion, she struggled to be free. "Stop," she said breathlessly, "I can't bear it."

The held each other tightly. "I want you," he said urgently. "It's torture to be with you and not be able to possess you."

"Tomorrow."

"One day without you is an eternity."

They stared at each other, their passion laced with despair.

"Marcus," she said huskily, "Perhaps it would be better if we said goodbye."

He looked at her, stricken. "Why?"

"The wedding," she said miserably. "That's what you should have. A bride. A wife."

"You."

Camilla shook her head. "Marriage can't ever happen for us. I'm trapped."

"I'll wait," he said stubbornly.

"There's nothing to wait for."

He gripped her arms and gave her a shake. "Hush, Camilla. I won't give up. Never. You're the only woman I'll ever love. I know you love me. And maybe," he said slowly, painfully, "maybe you're right, maybe we'll never be able to marry. But I don't care about that either. We love each other." His jaw jutted out. "We're tough, Camilla, you and I. We aren't going to give each other up."

She stared up at his bold face and determined mouth, and love swept her in such a flood she felt weak. Tears burned behind her eyes. He was wonderful. Perhaps she was greedy, demanding too much of the gods to expect to possess this man's love in perfection. Marcus was right. They were tough and they would love each other, love magnificently and gloriously and passionately as long as they could. She reached up and held his face, his dear face, and lifted her lips—

"Camilla."

Camilla turned a startled face toward the end of the arbor.

Cornelia ducked inside. "Papa's hunting for you."

"How did you know where I was?"

Cornelia smiled. "Phoebe loves you. She always knows where you are. She sent me to warn you."

Camilla looked nervously between her sister and Marcus, asked, "Cornelia, do you remember. . . ?"

Cornelia held her hand out to Marcus. "Of course, I remember Marcus," she said easily. "Rome's most sensational new lawyer. In fact, they were talking about you at the Emperor's last night."

Marcus bowed. "I hope the talk was kind."

"It was very complimentary. You're becoming a famous person." She paused, said in a low, suddenly serious voice, "If you will permit, I'll give you some advice." She glanced back over her shoulder.

Marcus looked surprised. "Of course. I'd appreciate that."

Cornelia bent close to him. "Don't go to very many parties at the Palace. It isn't a good place for you." She wasn't smiling and her eyes looked huge and somber. Then she said briskly, "Now, Camilla, you and I must see that everything's ready for the banquet."

As Camilla turned to go, Marcus whispered, "Tomorrow." Camilla nodded, but her mind worried at Cornelia's warning. What did she mean? What kind of danger did she foresee for Marcus? Camilla kept hoping for a word alone with Cornelia but friends and relatives were everywhere, in clumps in the reception hall, dotted throughout the courtyard now. At the banquet, Camilla was surrounded by a covey of cousins from Herculaneum. She saw Marcus at a distance and watched Cornelia talk to an old aunt who hadn't been in Rome in years.

Terentia and Sextus beamed with happiness. Camilla felt sure suddenly that there was genuine caring between Terentia and Sextus and her dear younger sister was sailing into a safe harbor. Camilla welcomed the joy of the day, but she couldn't forget Cornelia's warning to Marcus. What had Cornelia meant? Nothing truly serious, surely. Perhaps it was just that Cornelia liked Marcus, saw him to be decent and honorable and hoped he wouldn't get caught up in the kinds of debauchery the Emperor enjoyed. Cornelia didn't have to worry about that. Marcus wouldn't be tempted. Not Marcus.

Once again, the happiness that Marcus created in her brought a smile to her face. She wondered that all the people she talked to couldn't sense the delight that bubbled within her. Terentia wanted to know about love. Love was wonderful. Love was a glorious sweep of caring and joy, caring for another more than self, and joy in the glory of truly joining together.

An old friend, Senator Ligus, took her hand. "Camilla, I believe you're the prettiest woman in all of Rome. What did Decimus do to deserve you?"

"You're very kind, Senator," she said lightly. She looked past him. "Is your wife here today?"

The senator nodded and pointed toward the central fountain. "There's Livia. She never misses a wedding. Says it reminds her of ours. D'you know, I think that's a nice thing to say."

Camilla looked across the courtyard at the dumpy older woman with her hair flying in wisps and her double chins quivering as she talked excitedly to a friend. She looked back at the senator and saw him with new eyes. "Yes," she said slowly, "that's a very wonderful thing to say."

She moved away, her eyes thoughtful. That was love, too, love that spanned years, love forged in making a family. The older senator and his wife had seven children, a remarkable number in modern Rome.

Marcus should have the right to build a family.

But she and Marcus loved each other. They wanted each other passionately. For always.

Was she going to cheat Marcus of the kind of joy a man can have in his family?

"Camilla."

She whirled around and looked up at Marcus and she knew he saw the anguish in her eyes.

"What's wrong?"

She looked nervously around. Slaves darted past. Guests moved from group to group. "We can't talk here. I'll tell you tomorrow." She reached out and touched his hand, turned away. She knew he stood, looking after her.

Camilla moved among the guests the rest of the afternoon, smiling, talking, and all the while her heart ached. Marcus should have a wedding.

Could she bear to give him up?

The question nagged at her throughout the elegant banquet and she scarcely was able to eat though there was every delicacy offered during the many courses—doves and chickens, fish and lamb, olives, dates, almonds, chickpeas, and turnips, truffles, and copious amounts of wine.

As the sun set, guests gathered for the procession to lead the bride to her new home three blocks away which her father had purchased for his daughter and her husband. Terentia smiled shyly with quick, eager peeks at her new husband. In a flurry before leaving, she took a moment to hug Cornelia and Camilla, and Camilla carried with her Terentia's soft whisper, "I'm so happy, Camilla, so happy."

Camilla joined the jostling crowd, Decimus beside her. Boys carrying flaming torches led the way. The guests followed, singing and shouting rude jests. When the newlyweds entered their door and it closed behind them, the wedding day was done.

Slaves milled about seeking their masters. Decimus gestured at their litter-bearers. In the privacy of her curtained litter, Camilla jolted homeward, thinking of Marcus and of Senator Ligus and his wife.

She hurried into the reception hall, with no thought for Decimus until he called out for her to wait. Slowly, she turned.

"We've been invited to the Palace for a banquet next week." His voice was strained and tense and he stared at her intently.

Camilla looked at him curiously. "Oh?"

"We must go."

If he were truly her husband, she would want to know why they must go, but he was her husband in name only, and she didn't care. So she merely nodded, "Very well, Decimus," and turned and walked away. It didn't matter to her that they must go to the Palace. What mattered to her was Marcus and Marcus's happiness.

She lay awake most of the night. She couldn't give up Marcus. She'd rather give up life itself. But if she truly loved him, didn't she want him to have the best life he could? What kind of life was it for a man never to father a son or a daughter?

Camilla stared at the moving shadows on the wall. Tomorrow she would see Marcus. They must talk.

The next afternoon, Camilla had every good intention as she hurried up the steps to Marcus's apartment. Then the door swung open and Marcus reached out.

Before she could say a word, he pulled her into his arms and hugged her exuberantly. "I've missed you every moment. I dream about you whether it's day or night. Camilla, let me look at you." He tilted her face up toward his and the love in his eyes brought tears to hers. "None of that," he said quickly. "We're together. Don't let anything in the world take away from this moment."

She let him draw her inside. Before the door closed, their mouths met, eagerly, hungrily, happily, and Camilla lost herself in the ecstasy of loving him.

Marcus carried her to his bedroom. As he undressed her, he kissed her cheek, her shoulder, her breast. Her dress slipped to the floor and he pulled off his tunic. They lay together on his narrow bed.

Camilla stared into his eyes, dark eyes that held all the mystery and glory of life, eyes that beckoned her to come closer,

closer. She touched his cheek, ran her finger lightly over his lips. "You're beautiful," she said huskily.

He smiled, "A man is never beautiful."

"That's not true. You are beautiful to me."

"Not so beautiful as you are to me," he rejoined. "Your eyes are more glorious than the stars. Your mouth is sweeter than the softest flower. Your face has a lovelier glow than that of the moon."

"Oh Marcus, has anyone ever felt as we do?" She knew their words were extravagant, but they mirrored their feelings.

"Some few. Some very few."

His hands and his lips began to touch her, caressing her as lightly as a feather drifts in warm summer air.

Camilla reached out to him, her breath beginning to come quickly.

He laughed, softly. "Slowly, Camilla. Slowly, slowly."

The warmth of desire spread through her and she pulled him closer. "Marcus, now." They moved together, passion exploding like a towering wave as it rears high against the sky then thunders to shore.

When they lay quietly. Camilla touched his cheek. "Marcus," she said softly, "nothing in my life will ever be finer."

He smiled at her, his eyes warm and sleepy, his mouth curving gently. "Better and better, always, Camilla."

Happiness seeped from her face.

He frowned. "Why do you look sad?"

"Always means forever. We can't have forever."

He gripped her hand. "Listen to me. No one can count on forever. No one. We have now. That's all anyone can seek from life. Don't damage what we have by grieving for what we can't have. Don't give up. Something may happen."

She shook her head. Her throat ached as she tried to find

the words. "When I came today, I was going to tell you—" She broke off.

"Tell me what? His voice was stern.

"Someday you must have your son."

She saw pain in his eyes, but he pulled her close, wrapping his arms around her. His mouth moved against her cheek and he said fiercely, "Nothing matters to me as much as you. Don't torture me by threatening to go away."

"I want what's best for you."

"You are best for me." He kissed her, almost angrily.

Later, when they were dressed and he was walking her to the door, he asked, "Tomorrow?"

"Are you sure?"

"I'm sure."

"Tomorrow then, Marcus. Tomorrow for so long as you wish."

Relief brightened his face. "That's settled then. Camilla," he said hopefully, his eyes begging her to hope too, "sometimes the gods love lovers."

As her litter jolted up hill and down, Camilla rode behind closed curtains, absorbed in her thoughts. Marcus wanted her. For now. He loved her desperately. For now. She wanted his happiness more than anything else in life, so she would continue to meet him and to love him.

For now.

But if the day came when her love wouldn't be enough, she would know. When that day came, she would be ready. But now in the glorious, exciting, marvelous present, she was going to love him with all her being. Her mouth curved in a soft smile. She closed her eyes and relived the moments they'd just shared.

The litter stopped. "We're home, my lady."

Camilla pulled open the curtains. Felix helped her alight. She walked slowly into the house in no mood to surrender to these surroundings.

Decimus waited for her in the reception hall. "You've been gone all afternoon."

"Yes." She looked at him coolly. Why was he waiting for her? Why was he even aware of her absence. Her whereabouts had never mattered to him before.

Sunlight streamed from above, blinding her. She couldn't make out the expression on Decimus's face. But he leaned forward, reminding her unpleasantly of a coiled snake she'd once seen in a snake charmer's basket.

"I must talk to you." His voice was low and tense, utterly unlike his usual careless tones.

"I'm rather tired just now, Decimus. I've been to the Library. Perhaps before dinner . . ."

"I must talk to you now," he said harshly.

"Now?"

"Yes. Come into the study."

She followed him reluctantly.

Decimus gestured for her to sit on a couch.

Camilla took her place, looked up at him.

Decimus stood beside a table littered with papyrus rolls, several propped open. He appeared tired, almost haggard. And somewhat dissipated. He was losing the clear-cut handsomeness of his youth. Greyish pouches bulged beneath his eyes. Tight lines drew his mouth down. The years weren't being kind to him. She remembered his clear, fine face when they were married. She'd looked forward to becoming his wife, to loving him. At least she'd been spared that heartbreak. It would have been so much worse if he'd made love to her and to little boys, too. As it was, she could look upon him almost as a stranger. Except that he held so much power over her life.

He stood in the way of her ever achieving the life she dreamed about.

None of this was reflected in her voice when she spoke. "What is it, Decimus?"

He swallowed jerkily and she realized he was under a great strain. Abruptly, a pang of terror struck her. Did he know about Marcus? She waited, breath held, for his answer.

"I need money," he said flatly. "I need two million sesterces."

Whatever she'd imagined, it hadn't concerned money. Her tense muscles relaxed. "Two million sesterces? Whatever for?"

"I have enemies."

She looked at him thoughtfully. "What enemies?"

"The Jucundus brothers. Quintus wants to be governor of Syria. He's conspired against me."

Camilla raised an eyebrow. "A conspiracy?" She didn't quite laugh, but the idea was preposterous.

"You needn't look like that," Decimus said angrily. "It isn't a joke. I'm in terrible trouble."

"You'd better tell me."

"It would be better if you didn't bother your head about it. I wouldn't even mention it, but—"

"You have to have two million sesterces," she finished.

Two spots of white stood out on either side of his mouth. He hated asking her. Never before had it been necessary for him to approach her directly for money. She knew he'd borrowed from several bankers using her property for collateral. She'd signed for several loans for him. Until now, she'd accepted it as her duty. Decimus was her husband. But now, for the first time, he had to borrow directly from her. He had to have her approval, for she must instruct the freedman who managed her properties.

"I must know what the problem is, Decimus."

He radiated anger, his lips grimly set, his hands clenched.

She stared back at him, unrelenting.

Finally, he said shortly, "I fell into a trap."

"A trap?"

"The governorship in Syria. I did a good job out there. I built ninety miles of roads and pacified two communities. How could I have known Lucius Jucundus's brother was watching me like a hawk?"

It began to make sense. Lucius Jucundus was a well-known Roman lawyer. Any Roman lawyer or citizen could bring charges against anyone else.

"What did Lucius's brother find out?"

"It's all a lie," Decimus insisted. "A man's expected to make some money as governor. Everybody knows that."

"Are you accused of plunder?"

Decimus drew his breath in sharply. "It's a lie. But I've got to offer to pay the money back—when I'm tried."

As a senator, Decimus would be tried by the Senate if accused of a crime.

A sick feeling swept Camilla. "Are you going to be tried?"

"In a month."

Camilla knew the penalties for plunder. If convicted, Decimus could be sentenced to death or, if the Emperor felt lenient, banished to some faraway grim and desolate territory for years and years.

Camilla's family had never been associated with this kind of disgrace. Her father would be appalled.

Decimus's jaw jutted out. "I have to have the money, Camilla."

"I must look at the financial reports from my estates," she answered numbly. She got up from the couch and walked to the cabinet which held the monthly reports put together by her financial advisor. As she lifted down the most recent papyrus roll, she thought furiously. She didn't really need to check the reports. She'd studied them carefully on her return to Rome from the seashore. She had the money. More than enough money. It would take the yearly income from two villas, but that wasn't the real question in her mind. She was grappling with the daring possibilities Decimus's demand raised. For the first time in her married life, she was in a position of strength with Decimus. Now, if ever in her life, was the moment to seize the advantage.

She unrolled the papyrus and skimmed the figures. Actually, the Tuscany villa had shown its greatest profit ever this past year. The money was there. But she looked up at Decimus with a worried frown. "Two million sesterces is a great deal of money."

His eyes narrowed. "It will cost more than that if I'm convicted, Camilla. They can take half of everything I own."

That would be half of Decimus's property. Not hers.

He must have sensed her thoughts.

"Camilla, I've got to have your help. What's wrong with you?"

"Nothing's wrong with me. In fact, I'm glad to have this chance to talk with you. There are several things I'd like to discuss with you."

He jerked his head impatiently. "This isn't the time to worry about domestic problems. Whatever it is you want to do, new tapestries, free that old slave of yours, that can wait."

"No," she said quietly. "I want to talk to you."

"Talk about what?" he demanded shortly.

"About us, Decimus."

He tried to smile, but it wasn't a very good effort. His eyes were still angry. "I'm always willing to talk about us, Camilla. You know that."

They'd been married for seven years. She'd been a bride at fifteen like Terentia. The loneliness she'd endured since their marriage welled up inside her. She would have liked to scratch out his eyes. Anger and pain swept her.

She took a deep breath. "I'm willing to provide you with the money . . ."

He began to smile.

". . . providing that you divorce me."

Shock loosened the muscles of his face. He stood quite still. "Divorce you?"

"Yes."

After a long, strained moment, he began to smile again, an ugly, twisted smile. "I should have known you weren't a statue, Camilla. I suppose you've discovered all the interesting games Roman women play. Funny, I didn't think Publius Scipio's daughter would be interested."

She made no denial. "I had nothing in my home to hold me."

"That's true enough. I didn't take any time with you. Perhaps I should have." He saw the revulsion in her face. "So you wouldn't have liked that." He shrugged. "That's all right. I thought we had a pleasant arrangement, Camilla."

"I don't see that we had any arrangement at all," she said bitterly. "You've enjoyed the use of my money and the connection with my family. I've had nothing."

"Divorce," he said musingly. "Your father won't like it."

She stepped toward him. "But don't you see," she said eagerly, "if you divorce me, it will be all right."

His light-green eyes looked at her searchingly. "I begin to understand. You can be divorced in only two ways. If your father requests a divorce. Or if I request a divorce. We both know your father would never call for a divorce."

Camilla's chest ached. Would Decimus let her go? He had to have the money. Surely he would agree. Then she and Marcus could be together and her life could be the kind of life she'd always dreamed of. What was it Marcus had said? Sometimes the gods love lovers. Surely it was the gods that had put Decimus for once in her power.

He looked at her and once again smiled, a hating, hurtful smile and she saw, clearly and unmistakably, the cruelty in his soul. "No, my dear. I don't want a divorce. It's your duty to provide me with the money."

Camilla lifted her chin. "Understand me, Decimus," she said steadily. "I will be free. I'll never give you a penny unless you promise to divorce me."

A vein throbbed angrily in his throat. "You leave me very little choice."

"I leave you no choice."

Camilla heard her own words with shock. Could she actually be doing this, standing up to Decimus, demanding her freedom? She'd never in her life defied a man. And Decimus was angry, furiously angry.

She met his gaze unflinchingly.

His eyes fell away. "I have to have the money," he muttered, almost to himself. Then he nodded. "All right, Camilla. Have it your way." He grabbed up a slate tablet. "Here. Write out the instructions for your freedman."

"The divorce first."

He looked up at her, irritated. "Don't be a fool. I can't divorce you until the trial is over."

"Why not?"

"How would it look in the Senate if I divorced Publius Scipio's daughter? Word would get out, of course, that you were providing the money. Everyone knows what an admirable Roman matron you are," he said sarcastically. "I'd lose half the votes in the Senate."

Camilla bit her lip. She'd thought freedom might be minutes away, the freedom to love Marcus, to plan their wedding.

"I see." She took a deep breath. "You said the trial would be next month?"

"During the Ides of October."

One month. One more month and she and Marcus could be together, never to be parted. "As soon as the trial is over," she repeated.

"That's what I said. Now, write out the instructions."

Camilla took the slate and did as she was bid.

Decimus grabbed the slate. He scanned the writing and the tightness in his face eased. He was smiling when he looked at her and said smoothly, "You'll continue with your wifely duties until then, won't you?"

She looked at him uncertainly. "What do you mean?"

"I want you to come with me to the Emperor's party next week."

"I'll do that. Of course."

"Then I want to take my lawyer down to Swallow's Nest so we can work on my defense.

"You won't need me for that."

"It would look better. You like him."

"Who is your lawyer?"

"I'm going to get that young man who's making such a name for himself. The one who fished you out of the bay."

Camilla licked lips that seemed suddenly dry. "Marcus Paulus?" she asked.

"Yes. Marcus Paulus."

Somehow Camilla kept her face expressionless, but after Decimus left, she paced up and down in the study. Surely Marcus would refuse to take the case.

XI

The next day she worried all the way to Marcus's apartment. If Marcus took the case and lost it, it would make it impossible for them to wed. Surely Marcus had refused to defend Decimus.

They met at the top of the stairs. As soon as the door of his apartment closed behind them, they both burst into speech.

"Camilla, the strangest thing has happened."

She felt a flicker of despair. "Did Decimus come to you?"

Marcus nodded. "He came and he brought your father with him."

"My father?" This was worse than she could have imagined.

Marcus nodded. "Senator Scipio implored me to take the case. He said . . . well, he said some very nice things about my work." Marcus looked pleased and proud. "Camilla, your father's actually come to court and heard some of my cases."

"What did Father say?"

Embarrassed, Marcus repeated her father's praises.

"That's wonderful. I've never heard him say anything like that about another young lawyer."

Marcus frowned. "I didn't want to take Decimus's case, but your father begged me. He sees the accusations as a disgrace for your family."

"Did you take the case?"

"Yes. Camilla, do you mind?"

"I'm very much afraid of what might happen. Let me tell you what I've done."

Marcus listened with growing excitement. "He's promised to divorce you as soon as the trial ends?"

"Yes. Marcus, I can't help believing that the gods do love lovers."

"I told you, Camilla, we're meant to be together." He picked her up and swung her exuberantly around the room. "I intended to do my very best, Camilla, because I wanted to please your father. But now, well now I'll win the case no matter what it takes."

"Decimus wants you to come to Swallow's Nest with us."

His smile was huge. "I don't mind that either."

"You won't work in the afternoons, will you?"

He laughed and his arms tightened around her. "No, Camilla, never in the afternoon. Afternoons are for love." He kissed the tip of her nose. "It's afternoon now, isn't it?"

They walked arm-in-arm toward the bedroom, in no hurry for they were together. Soon, very soon, they would be one. But love on a sunny September afternoon when the air is soft and warm and smells of roses and honeysuckle is meant to be slow and tender with gentle whispers and soft caresses. They slowly disrobed. For a long, loving moment, they gazed at each other.

"You're beautiful," she said softly.

"No. But I'm very, very lucky."

Camilla touched his cheek, slipped her fingers lightly across his lips.

Marcus captured her hand in a gentle grasp and pressed his mouth against her palm. He kissed her palm, once, twice, a third time.

Camilla's heart began to race.

Marcus's lips touched her wrist, the inside of her elbow, her shoulder, and her neck.

Camilla moved into his arms. They held each other close, gently at first, then more and more tightly, their bodies hard against each other.

They spoke softly.

"Marcus, my love . . ."

"Camilla, heart's desire . . ."

When they lay together, Camilla twined her fingers in his thick, dark, curling hair and, boldly now, her mouth sought his. As passion pulsed through them, they strained to come together and there was nothing beyond the circle of their arms, not thought or danger, future or past, only this moment and its glorious burst of feeling, fast and quick and heated as water boiling in a cauldron.

Water glimmered emerald-green, reflecting the cavernous vaulted ceiling with inlaid panels of malachite. A stream splashed from the open mouth of a stone lion's head in the center of the pool.

Camilla stretched luxuriously, welcoming the pervading warmth. The silky touch of the water was almost as wonderful as the glorious warmth when she and Marcus made love. A smile of pleasure touched her lips. Could life ever be more wonderful than now? She had so much to look forward to, more than words could ever express or her heart could grasp. Years of love lay ahead, as shining as sunlight sparkling on waves, as breathtaking as the swoop of a hawk from a mountain crag, as satisfying as fresh cold water on a desert-hot day.

She turned around and around, delighting in the feel and freshness of the water. Then she wondered, idly, why Cornelia had asked her to come to the baths. Poor Cornelia. How dreadful to be bound forever in a loveless marriage and subject to the whim of an Emperor who daily became more infamous in the inner circles of Rome. Caligula had begun as Emperor only three years before, upon the death of Tiberius. The people welcomed Caligula, acclaiming him for his brilliance as an orator and his gentlemanly demeanor. But now stories swirled over Rome like autumn smoke. Caligula was cruel and greedy, caustic and prodigal, erratic and vicious.

Camilla frowned. Cornelia had warned Marcus to stay away from the Palace. Was there a particular reason or did her sister only hope to protect him from contact with the decadence that permeated Caligula's banquets?

Camilla floated for a moment on her back, then stroked lazily toward the deep end. She swam the length of the pool and clung to the side. When she saw Cornelia enter, she smiled and began to wave. How lovely Cornelia looked, tall and slim and regal with the bearing of a queen. It didn't matter what anyone said. She loved her sister and admired her.

Camilla's sense of peace fled when several women, mutual friends, ignored Cornelia's greeting and pointedly turned their backs.

Anger swept Camilla. How dare they? The fat, ugly wenches. None of them were good enough to sweep Cornelia's house. How dare they treat her so?

"Cornelia," Camilla called out loudly, her voice echoing in the cavernous room.

One of the women, the wife of one of Decimus's clients, looked toward Camilla in embarrassment. "Camilla, how are you today?"

"I'm fine," Camilla replied. "I'm going to swim today with my sister, Cornelia. Apparently you didn't see Cornelia come in."

The woman turned, laughing uncomfortably. "Hello, Cornelia."

"Hello there." Cornelia said it carelessly, but Camilla saw pain in her sister's eyes when she slipped into the pool beside her. "It's all right, Camilla. You don't have to fight them. I don't care."

"You do care," Camilla objected.

"Only a little. There are many other things in my life that matter more." She paused, said urgently, "Such as you."

"Me?" Camilla replied. Then she smiled, a smile of pure happiness. "Cornelia, I haven't seen you since everything changed. Let me tell you . . ." Her words tumbled out as eagerly as children running to play. She told Cornelia of Decimus's trial and the freedom she was buying. "I can't believe it's happened, but Decimus has promised to divorce me as soon as the trial is over." She looked shyly at her sister. "You know I love Marcus, don't you? I've not told anyone."

"I knew." Cornelia nodded, but her face was drawn, her gaze filled with misery. "I want you to be happy."

Camilla looked surprised at Cornelia's obvious distress. "I'm going to be happy. Didn't you hear what I said?"

Cornelia still looked grim. "You mustn't come to the Palace next week."

The abrupt shift in conversation disturbed Camilla. "How did you know I was going to be there?"

"I heard," Cornelia said. Her tone was strange. She leaned closer. "It's important. Don't come."

"I have to come," Camilla replied slowly. "I promised Decimus."

Cornelia's face twisted. "Damn him. Damn him to hell."

Cornelia's anger frightened Camilla. Cornelia took Camilla's hand, held it tightly. "You mustn't come." She licked her lips. "I don't want to tell you. You'll think I'm terrible."

"I could never think you were terrible," Camilla responded.

Anguish burned in Cornelia's eyes. "You have to understand, Camilla, I don't have a choice. If I don't do as Titus wants, he'll send the boys away. I can't lose my sons." Tears slipped down her cheeks.

Camilla slipped an arm around her sister's shoulders. "Don't cry, Cornelia. Whatever happens, you know I love you and I understand."

Cornelia shook her head miserably. "I was at the Palace last week," she said huskily. "On Wednesday. Always on Wednesdays. I was in Caligula's bed."

Camilla wanted to look away. She didn't want to see the pain that was her sister's face, but she watched and listened, held by the force of that deep, heartbroken voice.

"I won't tell you what he did. I don't want you to know. Ever."

"Shh," Camilla said soothingly. "I don't want to know, Cornelia."

"I have to tell you what he said," Cornelia continued raggedly. "He touched my face and said it reminded him of a statue of Aphrodite. The he said . . . he said . . . didn't I have a sister?"

Silence fell between them like a cavern, deep and full of dark things, unseen horrors.

"What did he mean?" Camilla asked finally, her voice thin and frightened.

Cornelia swallowed. "I tried to distract him . . ." Her eyes darkened.

Camilla knew she was remembering what she'd done and Camilla knew Cornelia suffered for her to try and turn the Emperor's mind away from a sister.

"He laughed." Cornelia struggled to get out the words. "Damn him. He said," and she spoke scarcely above a whisper, "'if you're this good, I certainly want to meet your sister.' He put his hand on my throat and squeezed and squeezed. I told him I had two sisters. He said, 'One of them I've heard about, the beautiful one.' I had to tell him. Camilla, I'm sorry." Tears streamed down her face.

"That's all right," Camilla said through dry lips, but fear quivered inside her. "It probably won't come to anything. He was probably just talking."

Cornelia stared blindly at a golden cupid in an alcove near them. "Perhaps."

Camilla took a deep breath. "I have to go to the Palace next week."

Cornelia's head jerked around. She stared at Camilla in despair. "You mustn't!" she cried.

"I have no choice," Camilla replied steadily. Horror ballooned in her mind. "Cornelia, do you think Decimus knows that the Emperor wants to meet me?"

Reluctantly, Cornelia nodded. "Decimus and Titus have spent a lot of time together lately. I think Titus told him how to please Caligula and that's why Decimus is insisting you come to the Palace."

Camilla stared down into the swirling green water. The warmth didn't touch her now. She felt encased in ice. Was there nothing Decimus wouldn't do to gain the Emperor's favor? Decimus knew, of course, that if Marcus lost his case in the Senate, his only hope would be an appeal to the Emperor.

Decimus was willing to barter her body for his future. That shouldn't surprise her.

"Pretend you are ill," Cornelia said urgently. "Camilla, you must."

If she didn't go to the dinner, Decimus could say their bargain was broken and he didn't have to divorce her.

"I have to go to the dinner."

A moan escaped Cornelia.

"I'll think of something." Camilla said reassuringly.

The days raced by, more quickly than birds beating their way to the south as the days shortened. The afternoon before the banquet, Camilla lay in Marcus's arms and wondered whether to tell him.

"You're very quiet," he said suddenly. He traced the shape of her face with his finger.

"Should lovers always share their thoughts?" she asked slowly.

He looked at her soberly, and she knew he was considering her question, holding it in his mind. That was another of the many reasons she loved him. He never dismissed her words with a shrug. She was his equal in mind and heart. She wanted abruptly to love him again, to kiss the corners of his mouth and to speak soft words meant for his ears alone.

"Not if it brings pain to the other," he said finally. He smiled, the gentle, loving smile Camilla treasured. "We don't have to worry about that, do we, my love? Every word you speak thrills my heart. Camilla, it won't be long now."

"No," she agreed quietly, "it won't be long now."

That afternoon as she rode in her litter toward home, fear once again crept up into her throat. What was going to happen at the Palace tonight?

At home, she paced up and down in her small bedroom. She felt alone, desperately alone. But she couldn't have told Marcus. He would be sickened and there was nothing he could do. What Caesar commanded, Caesar had.

If Marcus tried to thwart Caligula, he would not only fail, he would be in mortal danger.

But to think of Caligula's hairy hands touching her . . . To imagine the pressure of his angular legs . . . Camilla shuddered.

Her door opened. She swung around.

Decimus frowned. "Aren't you ready to go, Camilla?"

She stared at him. "Decimus, I don't feel very well."

"What do you mean?"

"I'm sick." She knew she must look ill, her face wan and drawn. "I can't go."

"You have to go."

All pretense had gone. His voice was hard and flat as the scrape of a soldier's boot on stone.

"If I don't?"

"You'll go if I have to carry you." His eyes blazed.

"What if Caligula finds me ugly?" she asked softly.

His face was hard. "You're beautiful even now, Camilla. He won't find you ugly. And you'll be honored, loved by a god."

Hatred quivered between them. Decimus would not even try to pretend. He didn't care what she thought or felt. He would do—and make her do—whatever was necessary for him to be saved.

She looked down at her hand mirror, its silver face lying upward on the bedside table. She could see her reflection, black hair upswept in shining curls, eyes huge and dark.

Camilla shivered. If the Emperor defiled her, how could Marcus ever love her again?

"You have experience now. Use your body to please him. It won't be that bad. Drink a lot of wine, Camilla. If it all works out, you can be sure I'll let you go. You don't have to tell your boyfriend, whoever he is."

Camilla took a deep breath and walked toward the door. When she stood even with Decimus, she looked deep into his eyes. "You are more despicable than anyone I ever knew." She pushed past him.

Outside, she ignored his helping hand when she climbed into her litter. "Don't touch me," she warned. "Don't ever touch me again."

Her litter jolted and swayed, tilted sharply upward. They were climbing the Palatine Hill. The Palace spread in extravagant glory on its summit. The street was jammed with litters. When they reached the Palace steps, trumpets blared as party-goers dismounted. Green, mauve, and blue gowns fluttered like evening moths among the shining white of togas. Immense bronze doors stood open at the top of a long flight of pale pink marble steps. This was the Palace. The heart of Rome. The Palace should stand for all that was great and good. Now it was a center of ugliness and vice. Beyond those doors, unspeakable orgies stained the nights.

Decimus gripped her arm, but she shrugged free. They moved along with the stream of banqueters. Camilla glimpsed Cornelia. Their eyes met and then Cornelia was out of sight.

The Emperor stood in the center of the reception hall. He wore a silk gown studded with emeralds and pearls.

Even in the midst of her fear, Camilla was struck by the magnificence of the hall and how that beauty was being defiled. The vaulted roof soared high overhead. Immense brightly-painted statues stood on pedestals in alcoves. Intensely white marble pillars supported the roof.

The Emperor waited on a dais. The Senators and their wives approached in twos.

Caligula stood with his chin high, the better to mask his balding head. Tall and pale, his broad forehead and hollow temples accentuated the thinness of his neck and legs. A loose smile stretched his broad mouth, but small, pig-like eyes looked cold as seaweed. He permitted the senators to reach up and embrace him, but he had eyes only for their wives. His wife, Caesonia, giggled happily beside him.

Camilla and Decimus stepped forward.

"Ah, Decimus," the Emperor remarked. "I understand you

made a great many friends in Syria." He smiled broadly. "They'd love to have you return."

A greenish pallor spread over Decimus's face. Camilla knew the words must have an ugly meaning.

Decimus bowed. "Your Highness, I'd rather serve you in Rome."

"My wish is your command," Caligula replied and his cold eyes glittered.

Decimus nodded.

"Isn't it?" Caligula asked sharply.

"Of course, Your Highness." Then Decimus said eagerly. "May I present my wife to you. You may think she looks familiar. Her sister is Titus Maro's wife."

Camilla heard him speak, knew she was being offered for the Emperor's pleasure. She and Decimus now were enemies and strangers, forever.

The Emperor's eyes traveled up and down her body. "I know your sister," and he put a salacious emphasis on the verb.

Camilla drew her breath in sharply, said stiffly, "My sister loves her sons."

Something moved in Caligula's eyes. A flicker of interest? Or anger? Camilla couldn't judge his response. If the gods were kind, she would never know him that well.

"Do you have sons?" the Emperor asked.

"No."

"Ah." He looked at Decimus and sniggered. "Perhaps that can be remedied. I'll talk to you later, my dear." He dismissed them.

Decimus gripped her elbow. Once again she pulled free of his grip, but walked with him into the huge banqueting hall. Several dozen tables, with couches on three sides, sat on the main floor. An ornately carved table of citron sat on a central dais. The three couches were built of cedar wood, the legs carved in the shape of dancing maids. Delicate, blue-veined marble topped the table. Silver serving dishes glistened in the flickering lamp light.

Slaves waited near each table, holding basins to wash guests' hands and feet.

Decimus spoke angrily, "Why did you say that to him? He can have you killed, you fool."

"That would be a shame," she retorted angrily.

"Camilla, you must do what he says."

"Must I? We'll see, Decimus."

Two other senators and their wives and three knights made up the group at their table. The wine, with only a splash of water, filled huge silver tumblers. Very soon, before the hor d'ouvres were finished, most of the diners were beginning to show the effects of too much wine.

"Drink your wine," Decimus ordered grimly, under cover of the babble of their table companions.

Camilla made no answer but turned the silver goblet round and round in place, not taking even a sip.

"Camilla, I order you to drink the wine."

She looked at him and it was he who dropped his eyes first.

The food, incredible even for a Palace banquet, came in wave after wave, snails and oysters, pheasants' tongues, tiny dormice rolled in honey and sesame seeds. The main course included baked pheasant, sturgeon in sauce, newborn kid, lamprey, mullet, and goose.

Camilla sickened at the sight of so much food.

The senator reclining next to her leaned close. His wine-sour breath flooded her face. "Where's your appetite, my sweet?"

"There's too much food," Camilla replied formally.

He shrugged. "Better eat today. Tomorrow may never come."

"Perhaps not," she replied, but he didn't hear, his wine-fogged mind already grappling with another thought.

Dinner seemed interminable, but Camilla dreaded its close. When the final serving was removed, slaves brought warm water scented with lilac. Camilla looked around, trying to see Cornelia, but the room was full and the flickering lights kept many of the tables in shadow. She couldn't find Cornelia.

The Emperor waved to his chief dining slave. The slave hurried to him, bent near, nodded once, turned to the musicians near the dais.

The sudden high staccato blare of a trumpet sounded above the mutter of laughter and conversation. Every face turned toward the dais. Almost every face looked fearful.

The Emperor smiled his loose smile. "I want to see all the women." He said it baldly with no effort at charm.

Camilla looked uncertainly at the wives reclining near her. One of them giggled drunkenly. Another bit her lip in concern. At other tables, women reacted in kind, some eager, some appalled.

The chief slave nodded at each table in turn. Slowly the women rose and walked in a single line toward the dais. Every so often, the Emperor called out and the line paused as he described the woman's attributes and conjectured aloud how she might perform. Every so often, he described clearly and distinctly how that woman had been when last in his bed.

Camilla tried not to listen. What would her father think if he saw this scene? He was a Roman and all Romans knew that Caesar ruled. Her father looked back with yearning to the days of the Republic when Romans ruled themselves. How far had they fallen that Caesar should publicly lust after senators' wives with never a word of protest from his subjects?

But Caesar ruled.

Then Camilla stood in front of the dais.

Camilla took one step, then another, and still he gestured.

Another step and another step until she stood across the table from him, so near she could see the stubble of beard on his chin, the glitter in his greenish eyes, the glisten of rings on his blunt fingers.

"You're very lovely. Fresh and new. How many men have you known, my dear?"

Camilla stared at him wordlessly.

"Answer."

Camilla swallowed, said in a thin whisper, "One."

Caligula tilted his head, careful to keep the balding top from view. "That's a shame. How would you like to know a god?"

Again her voice was a tiny reed of sound, but she was her father's daughter. "I would not like it."

Caligula frowned. Abruptly he distorted his face, bulging his eyes, puffing out his cheeks, twisting his mouth.

Camilla recoiled, a hand to her throat.

He laughed, huge, rolling guffaws.

The silence in the huge banqueting hall was intense. Not even the drunks moved or spoke.

The laughter pulsed against Camilla like a buffeting wind, harsh and shocking.

The laughter stopped. Caligula stared at her, his eyes hot and determined. "When Caesar speaks, the world obeys. Come with me."

The words reverberated in her mind, but she shut them away because she saw Marcus, his face white and sick, rising from a distant couch. Camilla lifted her hand as if to stop him and vertigo exploded within her. Her mind whirled like a thistle caught up by a dancing wind. Shards of color, red and purple and vivid green, moved within her mind then faded into a deepening black, thick and palpable as fur. She fell slowly, toppling down onto the marble floor, holding to a shred of consciousness.

Running footsteps slapped on the marble. Camilla heard Cornelia's voice. "Camilla's having another one of her fits."

Camilla's eyes fluttered and she looked up to see Cornelia leaning close to the Emperor, her brilliant red tresses swinging about her face. "You don't want a pale imitation anyway, do you, my lord?"

It was quiet in the garden outside the Palace.

Tears slipped down Camilla's face as she looked fearfully over Marcus's shoulder toward the Palace

"Don't cry, love," Marcus murmured, tightening his arms around her.

"My sister," she sobbed.

"Cornelia saved you."

"Marcus, it's hideous." She looked at him, tears smearing her vision.

Marcus nodded solemnly. "When you fell, I started for you, but Cornelia reached you first. At first, I was appalled, then I understood. She got his attention and I picked you up and said I was taking you outside for air."

Camilla remembered Cornelia's high laughter, and her offer of herself to Caligula. "Then she went off with him." Camilla's voice broke.

"She was brilliant." Marcus was somber. "Everybody knows Caligula hates the idea of fits. He won't bother you again."

"So he had Cornelia instead of me."

Marcus held her so tightly she almost couldn't breathe. "She's already traveled that road, Camilla. Accept what she's done for you. Now at least she can feel some of the ugliness was worthwhile."

"I can't repay her."

"She'll never ask you to."

Camilla clung to him. "My lovely sister . . ."

"I know," he said quietly.

"Camilla." The angry shout resounded in the garden.

Camilla and Marcus both stiffened.

The shout came again. "Camilla?" Decimus's voice was thick and slurred. "Are you out there?"

They stood silently.

"I don't want to see him," Camilla said grimly.

Decimus started to lurch down the stairs, then paused, peered into the gloom, swung his head uncertainly and turned to go back into the Palace.

Camilla looked up the graveled path that led between box hedges to the steps. "I want to get away from here."

"I'll call your litter. Tomorrow you must leave Rome."

"Yes." She knew she must be out of the Emperor's sight. "I'll go to the shore."

Marcus asked worriedly, "Will you have any trouble with Decimus?"

"Decimus . . ." She spoke his name vaguely, as if repeating a name from a distant past. "I'm not afraid of Decimus."

"You're sure?"

"I despise him. I don't fear him."

On the way home in the litter, she wondered if Decimus awaited her. But the reception hall was empty. She didn't ask the doorman if he had arrived. Instead, she walked quickly to her room and closed the door behind her. When the little slave girl came running to help her undress, Camilla sent her away. She didn't want to see anyone. Or talk to anyone. She dropped her gown on the floor and thought of her sister and the soft yellow gown Cornelia had worn this evening and how it must have lain crumpled on the floor of the Emperor's bedchamber.

Camilla turned restlessly in her bed. She mustn't think of

Cornelia. At least, she mustn't think of this night. But tears came as she slipped into sleep, crying for her sister and their yesterdays and their tomorrows.

The next afternoon, as the slaves scurried about packing for the journey to Swallow's Nest, Camilla stood in the study, facing Decimus.

"I'll go to the shore, but I don't want to talk to you again."

"You speak very strongly, Camilla."

"After last night, don't you wonder that I speak to you at all?"

He shrugged. "If you spread your legs for one, why not for another?"

"I suppose that seems reasonable to a man who uses little children. Anyone will do, is that right?"

They stared at each other, their faces taut and angry.

"Don't push me too far, Camilla. I haven't divorced you yet."

"We made an agreement. If you want the money, you must divorce me."

"All right." He was grim. "I'll keep my end of the bargain, but you must, too. You must come to the villa and you must treat my lawyer decently."

Nothing moved in her face and eyes. "I have great regard for Marcus Paulus," she said simply.

It was an odd journey with Marcus accompanying them. Each night, when they stopped at friends' villas along the Appian Way, Camilla and Marcus spoke very formally. Occasionally, for a fleeting moment, he would touch her hand or his eyes would meet hers, and a song sang in her heart.

On the last day of the journey, she leaned forward eagerly as Swallow's Nest came into view. It had never looked lovelier. Her villa. Once again she felt the villa to be hers alone. Decimus was an interloper, soon to be gone. One day not too far distant she and Marcus would walk together as they had that very first time, the wind sweeping against them from the sea, their hearts racing from exertion and love. They would come to the villa and there would be children, their children, and, once again, high voices would repeat lessons on sunny summer mornings.

Holding fast to her secret hopes for the future, Camilla managed to treat Decimus civilly. Once they reached the villa, she saw him only at dinner. Every morning, she heard Marcus arrive and join Decimus in the study. She felt closed away from Marcus, alone, lonely.

But, in the afternoons . . .

XII

The water slapped cheerfully against the cliff face. Marcus took Camilla's hand. "Come down this path. I'll show you a secret place for us."

They scrambled down the cliff, skidding a little as the faint path steepened, clutching the rock face and each other, once bringing up hard against a boulder to keep from tumbling into the pool below, laughing together.

"Marcus, you fool, we're going to fall."

"Who cares? I'd love to see you with your dress all wet against you. Here," and he picked her up in his arms and held her over the drop.

"I'll take you with me," she warned.

"Of course."

"Marcus, you're silly."

He kissed her then, once, twice, eagerly, gently, and she tasted him and the salt air and the playful breeze off the sea.

"You smell good," he murmured.

"Lilac perfume," she said softly, her mouth against his cheek, but she wasn't listening to her words, she was delighting in the feel of his skin against her lips and the wiry coil of his thick black hair beneath her fingers.

Slowly, he swung her back to the path. They stared into each other's eyes.

"I'd like to shout your name," he said softly. "I'd like to climb to the top of a mountain and call out 'Camilla, Camilla!'"

"We could climb together."

"We'll climb together." His words came more and more slowly and it didn't matter what he said because the look in his eyes told her everything. His gaze held love and a promise and desire. Slowly, they moved into each other's arms and she welcomed the feel of his body against hers, the warmth and pressure. They held each other tightly for a long moment. Then Marcus led her around a pinnacle of rock and down a few more feet where the path ended at the shadowy mouth of a cave. Water moved up and down only a few feet below the cave entrance, hissing and slapping, a gentle, constant refrain.

Camilla slipped free from her gown. Marcus dropped his tunic onto the cave floor, knelt to spread it over the sand and pebbles. He reached out for her. His lips touched her knee, her thigh. She sank down onto the pallet. In the shadowy air, their limbs gleamed like garden statuary at dusk. They called each other's names in husky half breaths until their mouths met and held and then the magic swept them and they came together in a rush, and there was nothing in life but his moment.

When they lay quietly together in each other's arms, their faces almost touching, Camilla said softly, "I love you, love you, love you."

He smiled. "We're going to have a wonderful life together."

She reached out, gently touched his lips. "Shh, Marcus."

He looked puzzled. "Why can't I talk about how wonderful our life is going to be?"

"Don't say it. It makes me afraid."

"Afraid? Why?"

She bit her lip. "I don't know exactly. But I know that no one in the world has ever loved like we have and I'm afraid the gods may be jealous."

A cool brush of wind curled around the rock, touching them, foretelling evening.

He didn't laugh. Instead, he nodded soberly. "I understand. Sometimes, I'm afraid, too. You're right. We won't talk about our future." He paused, said boyishly, "I can't help counting the days."

The afternoons came as surely as sunrise and sunset, and Camilla wondered at the glorious possibilities of love, always new and different, exciting and fulfilling. Some days they made love. Other days they talked, sometimes of literature, sometimes of friends, sometimes of the wonders of starfish or the moon or poetry.

One afternoon, she studied Marcus almost as if she'd never seen him before. They sat on the rocks outside the cave. Sunlight glistened on his dark, strong face with its bold nose and firm mouth. He looked toward her, his dark eyes full of desire. Marcus pulled her toward him.

"We must go into our cave," she said breathlessly.

"No one can see us here among the rocks," he said urgently.

There was just room for them to lie together. Camilla looked up into Marcus's face. His black hair shone a deep blue black.

"Like a panther," she murmured.

His lips touched hers for a fleeting instant. "A panther?" He kissed her again.

"You," she said softly. "You are strong and lithe and graceful."

Her words fell away because there was no more room in her mind for words, only feelings, as his lips touched the corner of her mouth, her chin, her nose, her eyebrows. Her hands slipped up his back and she felt the strength of his muscles. She kissed him in return. He made a low, soft sound, then their mouths came together and it was the same yet always different, a pulsing explosion of sensation. She felt his hands low on her hips, lifting her up to him, and she came eagerly.

The sunny September afternoons slipped away, each perfect in its own fashion. Camilla's heart began to race each day as the sun arched midway in the sky and she hurried up the path to the headlands, knowing that soon she would be with Marcus.

Nothing could match the delight of these afternoons, but the anticipation of love and the actuality of love accentuated each other. She knew without doubt that no two lovers ever enjoyed a September more. And each day they were coming nearer to a long life filled with love.

Only a few more days . . .

Waves splashed against the cliff face.

Camilla knelt on the edge of an upturned slab of rock and reached down to touch the water. She shivered. "The water is terribly cold, but I love it."

Marcus lazily caressed her hair. "Why is that?"

Camilla slapped her hand against the water and watched it form a lacy curtain before falling away. "Cold water always reminds me of you."

"I like that," he said playfully. "I must be a wonderful lover if I make you think of icy water."

"The water was so cold when I fell that day," Camilla replied. "Cold and dark and I thought that was what death was like, then, suddenly, I felt your arms around me. Now, no matter what happens, I know your arms are waiting."

He took her in his arms and held her so tightly she could feel the beating of his heart. But there was a touch of desperation in his grasp.

"Camilla, promise me you'll always be mine."

"Always."

"We go back to Rome tomorrow," he said solemnly.

"I will love you in Rome or here or anywhere I am in the world."

He smiled, then almost at once sighed.

"What's wrong?"

He shook his head a little. "I don't know. I'm ready for the trial. I feel it's a test. If I win, I'll have you. If I don't—"

"You'll win."

"I think I will," he agreed slowly, "but I hate for our time here to end."

"Don't feel that way. Every day that passes brings us closer to the time when we can be together forever."

"I know. But this month has been perfect. I wish we would stay here for-ever, you and I."

"You'd miss Rome, the courts, the excitement."

He looked at her gravely. "When I came home from Greece, I wanted more than anything in the world to be a great orator, like your father. Now everything's different. I want to be a lawyer, but nothing matters as much as you."

Tears glistened in her eyes. "Marcus," she whispered, "whatever happens to us, I'll never forget your saying that."

The next day, as the litters jolted slowly northward, Camilla thought of their final moments alone together on the rocky ledge above the sea. A wave of melancholy swept her that those afternoons were now beyond recall. She tried to shake away her depression. In only a few days, they would be in Rome, then, once again, in the afternoons, she and Marcus would spend happy hours together. And soon, oh, count the days, he would argue at Decimus's trial, then she would be free.

Decimus had promised her the divorce if she gave him the money to make restitution to the provincial government.

It was all agreed upon.

Settled.

Nothing could go wrong.

"I'm going to denounce Cornelia." Her father spoke harshly, implacably, but his lips trembled.

"Papa, calm yourself. Please. You don't know what you're saying."

Senator Scipio reached out and gripped the wooden frame of the arbor. The knuckles of his hand whitened with pressure. "I told you, Camilla." The words sounded hollow and cavernous, as if he barely had the strength to speak.

Camilla looked down at the fountain. The water gurgled cheerfully, spouting in a high, silky arch from the central pipe. The garden smelled of autumn, of dry and dusty leaves that crackled underfoot. The last roses of summer shed their petals like slow-falling tears.

"You can't believe everything you hear," Camilla pled.

Her father shook his head and looked at her, his eyes dulled with misery.

Camilla licked dry lips. "People are jealous of Cornelia. She's so beautiful."

"I wish she'd never been born."

"Papa, please don't say that."

"I have to say the truth. My daughter—a whore."

"No." Tears burned Camilla's eyes.

Her father reached out and pulled her close to him. "Camilla, Daughter, I'm sorry I told you. I shouldn't have told you."

He hadn't been able to bear the pain alone; Camilla understood that. He'd burst into the Roman house the afternoon Camilla arrived, his eyes wild and feverish, his voice hoarse.

Camilla reached up to pat his cheek. "Papa, I don't care who told you, I don't believe it. I don't believe any of it." She heard her words with a sense of shock. This was the second time she'd lied to her father. Both times, she lied for Cornelia.

This time he didn't believe her.

He wanted to believe her. She saw the tiny quiver of hope in his eyes, then he said harshly, almost shouting, "I heard the man. I heard him with my own ears."

His face ashen, he told it again, as a man rubs at a wound, picks at a sore, making it hurt more and more. "I was at the Baths of Agrippa. That's where the word gets around about women. But this time, it's my daughter and there's no mistake about it. It was that chariot driver, the Greek one, Demetrius. He drives for the Greens." His voice rough and uneven, he described the team and its victories and Demetrius, the hero of the moment in Roman society for his string of 64 victories. "He stood there and showed the muscles in his arms," the senator continued bitterly. "That's the kind of man he is. Then one of his friends asked, "Who's the redheaded wench who almost made you late for the races yesterday, Demetrius?" and he answered . . ." Camilla's father swallowed thickly. "He said, 'She's a senator's wife and a senator's daughter, Cornelia Scipio, and she's better in bed than any woman I've ever had.'"

The words fell between them.

Camilla's father stared at her for a long moment, then he said with a bitter finality, "I'm going to denounce her."

"Papa, wait. Let me talk to Cornelia."

"It's too late for talk, Camilla."

"Papa, sometimes things can look much worse than they are."

He shook his head.

Camilla clutched his arm and it was as hard and unyielding as a rock. "Papa, promise me you won't do anything until I talk to Cornelia."

"Why?"

She saw the sorrow and pain in his eyes. He felt he must do his duty and it was a father's duty to denounce a wanton daughter if her husband refused to do so. That was the Roman way. The old Roman way. Augustus denounced his daughter Julia and banished her for life to a tiny, barren island and forbade her to have any men friends at all. In the Rome of today, fathers and husbands looked the other way.

"Papa, Cornelia loves her sons."

"If she loves her sons, she should behave as a Roman matron," he said in that terrible voice. Yet, once again, his mouth trembled.

"Papa, have you never made a mistake? Never, in all of your life?"

He drew himself up to his full height. He'd never looked more imposing, his craggy face rock hard. His toga fell in perfect folds as a Roman senator's should. He wore it without apparent effort despite its heavy weight. "I was always faithful to your mother and she to me."

"I know that," Camilla said quickly. "But think of your whole life, Papa. Have you never made a mistake, erred in some way?"

He was quiet.

Camilla waited. As she waited, she made a small prayer.

"Many years ago," he said haltingly, "I accused a senator of dishonesty. I prosecuted him. He was convicted and stripped of his properties. He opened his veins at the Emperor's command." He sighed heavily. "I discovered I was wrong. The thief was his brother."

"You made a mistake," Camilla said gently.

Her father nodded. "I paid his widow for his estates out of my own monies. Yes, I was wrong."

"No one could bring him to life again." She hated saying it, hated seeing the distress in his eyes. But she had to fight for Cornelia with any weapons she could find.

"I couldn't bring him to life again."

"Papa, don't you see? Sometimes, we can be wrong, we can be told things that aren't true. Please, let me talk to Cornelia. Perhaps, if she promised to go to her villa in the mountains for a year, then the talk that's going around will stop. People will find something else to gossip about."

He looked across the garden, but Camilla knew he wasn't seeing the final glorious flowering of the roses or the glittering bits of stone in the mosaic around the fountain. He was seeing Cornelia and, through her slender and lovely face, recalling the delicate beauty of his beloved wife. Camilla waited, watching his face anxiously. He would see through her offer, of course. No one would ever say that Senator Scipio was stupid or obtuse. Obviously, persuading Cornelia to leave Rome for a year would only mask the problem of her promiscuousness, not remove the stain from the family. Cornelia leaving for a year would beg the real question entirely. But did he really want to denounce his oldest and loveliest daughter? Did he really want to bring everlasting disgrace to her name? Did he want to separate Cornelia forever from her sons?

Would he, Camilla prayed, just once in his life bend from the rectitude for which he was famed?

He stared down at the ground, his face furrowed. Finally, gruffly, he said, "I'll wait until you talk to Cornelia." He looked at his middle daughter, misery and despair in his eyes. "You understand she must leave Rome for at least a year. She must free herself from any suggestion of wanton behavior. Forever."

"Of course, Papa."

He turned on his heel and walked away. Camilla stared after him, her heart aching. But she may have fashioned a way out for Cornelia. Could her scheme possibly work? Would the Emperor permit Cornelia to leave Rome? How could Titus be persuaded to agree? But Cornelia must go. If she didn't leave Rome, her father would denounce her.

Camilla pressed her hands against her cheeks in distress. It might bring danger to their father if he insisted upon denouncing Cornelia and the Emperor wanted her near.

Camilla's hands dropped and she paced back and forth by the fountain. She'd bought time for Cornelia. Perhaps, after she talked to Cornelia, they could come up with another plan, something to satisfy their father yet not put Cornelia in opposition to either the Emperor or her father.

Camilla looked at the sun dial. It was already the fourth hour after sunrise. Perhaps she could catch Cornelia at home. She rehearsed what she was going to say as her litter bounced and jolted along. At Cornelia's house, she hurried into the reception hall.

The house steward greeted her. "The mistress isn't home this morning."

Camilla frowned. "I must talk to her. Where is she, Primus?"

The steward paused, said without expression, "The mistress is at the Games today. With the Emperor's party."

A wave of shock washed over Camilla. Cornelia at the Games. Their father had always opposed the Games. He called them barbaric and sickening. All her life, Camilla had heard of the combats, gladiators against criminals, animals against slaves. She'd never gone. Few women of their class attended, except, of course, the Vestal Virgins who sat in a special box near the Emperor. Also, the Emperor's party could include women. Otherwise, only low-born women attended the games, sitting high along the rim of the amphitheatre, segregated from the men.

Camilla turned and walked outside. She climbed into her litter. When her chief bearer asked their destination, she said brusquely, "To the Games."

For once a slave's impassive face revealed surprise before the smooth mask of obedience returned. "Yes, Mistress."

He would know the way, of course. Notices went up days in advance, announcing the appearance of famous gladiators and exotic animals. They were still blocks away when she heard the roar of thousands of voices, rising higher and higher to end in frenzied screams. Camilla felt a sense of horror, but she had to talk to Cornelia. Without delay.

As her bearers wormed their way through the crowd jammed around the amphitheatre, Camilla looked in dismay at the packed sweating mass of humanity.

"Make way," her chief slave shouted. "Make way for a senator's wife."

Grudgingly, men stepped back, opening a wedge of space.

Near the entryway, the chief slave leaned close. "This is as near as we can get, Mistress."

Camilla nodded and dismounted, well aware of his veiled curiosity. "Wait here for me," she ordered curtly. Head held high, she walked toward an entrance. The men, mostly plebeians, made way for her, but a little murmur of curious talk swirled after her. "Who's that?" "A senator's wife," somebody said. "Going to the Emperor's box?" A hoarse laugh. "She doesn't look like that sort."

Camilla's cheeks burned but she kept going. She plunged gratefully into the coolness beneath the stone arches. The scent of wine and bread and fruit emanated from stalls. Camilla started up a wide ramp. Once again, louder and even more chilling, shouts erupted from thousands of throats in a mind-numbing roar. Camilla looked up toward the splotch of light that marked the opening to the seats. Camilla felt sick, almost faint, but she must keep on. She was almost to the top when a guard barred her way. "No women here. You'll have to take the next ramp, then the stairs to the top."

"I'm going to the Emperor's box."

"Oh, sorry, my lady. If you'll give me your marker."

"Marker?"

He looked embarrassed, but persisted. "The ladies going to the Emperor's box have a marker."

Camilla shook her head. "I don't have one." She hesitated, said pleadingly, "I will only be there for a moment. My sister is there and I must speak to her."

"Not without a marker," he said gruffly, and he barred the way.

Camilla turned and started up the next ramp. Breathless, she reached the top of the amphitheatre just as a thundering of hooves exploded in the hot afternoon air. She struggled past a tightly packed group of women, many smelling of sweat and wine, and strained to see below. A brilliant expanse of white glittered beneath her, massed togas gleaming in the vivid sunlight. Paler blobs marked faces. As if moved by puppeteers, the faces changed, mouths opening, voices roaring, louder than the crash of ocean waves. Shouts beat against her mind and she heard, too, the high anguished squeal of the horses as they galloped and wheeled around the arena, trying to escape the fangs and claws of the hunger-maddened black panthers loping after them. One panther crouched, muscles rippling across his glistening black back. In a flashing blur, he launched himself into the air and landed on a chestnut mare's back. The terrified horse reared and bucked, but the panther clung tightly. His gleaming black head moved and his teeth sank into the horse's neck. Blood spurted in a curving arc, spraying the sand-covered floor of the arena. The mare fell to her knees, sagged onto her side. The panther ate greedily. Other horses thundered by but none could escape the panthers.

A clean-up crew ran onto the arena floor and began to pull away the carcasses of the dead horses and shoo the live ones out. A panther watched intently then jumped on one of the custodians. The crowd laughed and cheered.

Camilla shuddered and looked away from the twitching body of the custodian. From this height, the people in the lower levels of the amphitheatre looked like tiny gesticulating dolls. There was the Emperor's box. Cornelia sat beside him. Even from here, Camilla could see the tenseness of Cornelia's body. Cornelia was delicate and gentle. How she must hate what she was seeing.

Sound swept the amphitheatre again. As the clean-up crew finished spreading fresh sand over the bloodied markings left by the mauled horses, huge gates clanged up at the end of the arena. A gigantic man, well over six feet tall, strode out. He raised a shield and sword above his head. The cheers rose to a crescendo.

"Lucius, Lucius," the crowd chanted.

Even Camilla knew his name. He was the libertine son of a famous family, known for his violence and viciousness. He had taken the life of a gladiator and he was credited with seventy-two kills. The crowd loved him. They moaned his name in an ecstasy of excitement.

Who would he face today?

Lucius raised his face toward the sun and spread his arms so that all could see the breadth and strength of his chest. His powerful legs looked like pillars of stone. He swung his sword in an arc above his head.

The crowd cheered again. Their hero was here. Who would he kill today? How would it happen?

Camilla had seen him once at a party. His swarthy face bore a livid scar on one cheek. He lacked one ear. Other scars marred his arms. Most of all, she remembered his eyes, dark and restless, and his huge hands.

The gates clanged at the other end of the arena. The crowd gasped in surprise, then laughed in delight. Five blunt-bodied little men, Numidian dwarfs, ran out. Bright patches of color marked their dusky backs and chests. Each carried a spear.

"Lucius," the crowd screamed again.

The dwarfs paused in a semicircle. The little man in the center of the curved line raised his spear. The dwarfs moved toward the gigantic gladiator.

Lucius gave a bored shrug. He poked his sword into the sand and casually leaned on it.

The black dwarfs paced nearer and nearer. The crowd shouted, "Kill, kill, kill." The dwarfs moved like a line of dancers, pausing after every step. They looked like a strange animal, a creature from the ocean floor.

Abruptly, with no warning, Lucius plunged forward, flailing his sword to the right and the left, charging the line of dwarfs. Catching them by surprise, his swinging sword severed the heads of two of them. He burst through their line, turned to face them. The heads thumped into the sand, and blood spewed from the cut jugular veins, drenching Lucius and the surviving dwarfs. Lucius tucked his shield beneath his arm and used his free hand to wipe blood from his chest. He raised the stained hand to his lips and took a taste. He looked up at the crowd and raised his clenched fist.

That glance upward, that arrogant gesture, cost him dearly.

The smallest dwarf, who appeared to be about three feet tall, turned as his comrades fell. He threw his spear. The spear landed in Lucius's chest with the solid sound of an axe cracking a tree. The gladiator stood for a moment, bloodied fist still raised high. Slowly, like a toppled oak, he sank to his knees. He didn't fall.

Another dwarf ran toward him and lodged his spear in Lucius's side. The dwarf used both hands to push the spear deeper.

Lucius thudded to the ground.

The crowd roared again but in anger now. The little Numidians had killed their hero. The spectators shouted their fury. Every head turned toward the Emperor's box. It was the Emperor's choice whether victorious fighters should live or die. Caligula listened to the calls for death. He turned to Cornelia and whispered in her ear. The crowd's shouts grew. Slowly, Cornelia raised her hand with the fingers clenched and the thumb pointed to the sky. The crowd screamed in anger. The Emperor shook his head. Slowly, Cornelia turned her fist down, her thumb pointed to the ground.

The surviving dwarfs raised their hands in a plea, but the custodians yanked away their spears and trussed the little men to poles jammed quickly into the ground. The custodians painted the dwarfs with pitch then lit flaming torches. As they walked toward the bound men, one of them began to scream. Camilla clapped a hand over her mouth and turned away, struggling through the jam of women to the exit.

She smelled blood and burning flesh as she ran down the ramp. Tears streaked her face. She cried for the men and the animals and for her sister, whose down-turned thumb had sentenced the little men to a hideous death. Camilla plunged out of the amphitheatre and looked for her bearers. They jumped to attention when they saw her. Camilla climbed into her litter and said huskily, "Take me to the Campus Martius, to the shop of Aristides the jeweler."

Again, the slave's impassive face betrayed no surprise. He nodded. Camilla knew he wondered. She didn't care. Let him think what he would. She must see Marcus.

XIII

Marcus held her in his arms as she told him about the panthers and the horses, the gladiator and the dwarfs, and Cornelia's thumb. Rackingly, violently, Camilla vomited into a basin. Marcus steadied her quivering shoulders. When she could heave no more, he used a cool, wet cloth to wipe her face.

Finally, Camilla wept. "I'm sorry, Marcus."

"Sorry? What do you mean?" he asked gently.

"To be sick. To be ugly when I'm with you."

He turned her face to make her look at him. "Did you think I'd only love you in the good times?"

Once again tears brimmed in her eyes, but these were tears of joy.

"You and I," he continued firmly, "are going to meet everything together. The good and the bad."

"Marcus, why am I so lucky?"

"Lucky?"

"Lucky enough to have met you."

"I'm the lucky one," he responded.

For the first time in hours, she smiled. The horror would never leave her memory but she once again felt as if she were in a world with goodness, too. Being with Marcus was a world away from the amphitheatre. The harsh shouts demanding death couldn't penetrate here. Here there was decency and gentleness.

He pulled her to her feet. "Come with me, Camilla. I know what will make you feel better."

Uncertain, she followed him to the apartment door, then hesitated.

"It's all right." His voice was reassuring. "These are private stairs."

"Where are we going?"

"Downstairs behind Aristides' shop, there is a private bath house."

"I can't go to a bath with you."

"This bath is truly private. When you came, I saw you were upset. When I went to get a cool cloth for you and a basin, I sent my manservant down to reserve the bath for me."

She followed him down the stairs and into the bath entryway. It was patterned after the huge baths but built on a small scale. The mosaic floor glittered with tiny dots of gold scattered among blue and black stones. Porpoises cavorted cheerfully in a green and gold mural on the walls. Marcus took her hand and they entered the dressing area. Camilla looked around, but they were absolutely alone. It was utterly quiet and private. She loosened the brooch that fastened her dress.

As they stacked their clothes in the stone cubicles, they smiled at each other.

"Camilla, you are more lovely than Aphrodite."

Camilla smiled, knowing it was a lover's exaggeration but such welcome words when she felt soiled by the morning's horrors. And she thought of the old senator who had spoken to her at Terentia's wedding. "Will you love me still, Marcus, when I am old?"

"You will never be old to me," he replied. He reached out then, his fingertips just touched hers. They walked, loosely linked but exquisitely aware of each other, into the warm room. Water swirled in a shallow basin in the center of the room. Overhead, bronze Cupid smiled as they held garlands of flowers. Sunlight streamed through a high broad window in the western wall.

Marcus scooped up a handful of warm water and gently splashed her. They stood close together, near but not touching, and doused each other. Soon their bodies glistened wetly. She pushed away all thought of the morning. Being with Marcus made her feel clean and whole again. There was goodness when they were together. Together they created a circle where evil couldn't enter.

They walked into the central room where a pool with blue and green tiled borders held sunlit water that lapped gently against the sides.

She started down the steps, paused to look back at him.

"Go on. I want to see you with your hair streaming behind you and the water around you."

She slipped into the water and floated on her back. He stood above her at the edge of the pool and she loved the pleasure and excitement in his eyes.

"Come here," she said urgently. "Come be with me."

He jumped lightly in the pool. They came together in the waist deep water and molded their bodies together. She raised her mouth hungrily to his and held him tightly. They kissed, and the warmth of their passion and the warmth of the water made her gasp his name. She called his name over and over again. He waited until she cried out and then he was within her.

They found a bench carved just beneath the water level in the shallow end and stretched out on it together. Marcus held her in the circle of his arms. The water swirled gently around them, and her long black hair wavered.

"Each time we make love," Camilla said softly, "I think this time is the best, that it can never be as wonderful again. Every time is more wonderful."

Marcus kissed her cheek. "Our love will always be more and more wonderful. Camilla."

"I don't understand how that can be so."

"That's what love is like."

She looked at him sharply. "You say that so confidently. How do you know so much about love?"

He laughed. "Are you jealous, thinking I've loved someone else and that's how I know?"

She looked at him in an agony of wondering.

"Don't worry, Camilla. I've never known love like this." He frowned thoughtfully. "I understand what you mean. Every time I hold you, every time I possess you, I think it can never be so marvelous again. Every time it is even better. That's how I know it will always be so."

She kissed the tip of his blunt chin, loving the tiny feel of bristle. "I never understood until now about the magic that holds a man and a woman together. That is the reason, isn't it?"

He nodded. "Soon, very soon, we can make love in our own home."

They swam together, their bodies so close.

Finally, as sunlight slipped up the east wall, Camilla said quietly, "I must start home soon."

They lingered at their dressing, but the minutes sped. Camilla looked more and more distressed.

Marcus understood. "When are you going to talk to Cornelia?"

"Tomorrow. Early." Camilla bit her lip. "I'm afraid I've made a mess of it."

"You've staved off action by your father."

"Only for a little while. He will still denounce her if she doesn't leave Rome for a year. I'm afraid the Emperor won't let her leave. Even if the Emperor agrees, Titus will be opposed because he wants Cornelia to please the Emperor for his own advancement." Camilla pressed her hands against her cheeks. "There's no way out."

Marcus frowned. "I have an idea." Slowly, then more quickly as his thoughts crystallized, Marcus sketched a plan.

Camilla listened intently, burst out, "Do you really think that could work?"

He looked at her confidently. "Yes."

It all depended upon her.

"I'll do it," she said firmly.

The next morning, as she alighted from her litter at Cornelia's, she wished Marcus were with her. She could scale mountains or slay tigers with Marcus at her side. But he had crafted a way. It was up to her to make it work.

Cornelia was still abed. Camilla brushed aside the slave girl and opened the bedroom door.

"Get out of here," a thick voice ordered. "Get out." A glass decanter of perfume thudded into the wall beside the door and broke. The sweet scent flooded out as shards of glass tinkled to the floor.

Camilla hurried across the floor.

Cornelia huddled in her bed, the loose top cover wadded and rumpled, face hidden in cloth. She mumbled, "Get out."

"Shh, Cornelia, it's me, Camilla. Shh." She dropped down beside the bed and gently touched her sister's shoulder.

Cornelia rolled over, stared up. Her face was pasty and swollen. "The light hurts my head. I feel awful."

Camilla smelled the sour odor of wine. "I know," she said gently.

Cornelia pressed her fingers against her temples and moaned. "No," she said dully, "you don't know, Camilla. Not even in your worse nightmares can you imagine. Yesterday, I had to go to the Games with the Emperor." She shuddered. "I don't know," she said raggedly. "Perhaps I will open my veins. I can't bear what has happened to my life. It's hideous."

Camilla held her sister tightly. "I know. I was there yesterday, Cornelia."

"At the Games?" Cornelia looked up at Camilla. In the morning light, Cornelia's lovely face was ravaged and worn. "You were at the Games?"

"I came to try and find you."

"Why?" Cornelia asked blankly.

Camilla looked at her sister's pain-wracked face and knew she was going to wound her sister more. She had no choice. "I have to talk to you, Cornelia. You see, Papa . . . Papa's heard . . . he's heard . . ."

"About me?" Cornelia struggled to sit up. Tears trembled in her eyes. "I will kill myself!" she cried wildly.

"Wait, Cornelia, hear me out."

"Is he going to denounce me?" Cornelia's face twisted. "I'd gladly be banished to the ends of the earth to be free of the Emperor. But Caligula won't permit me to leave Rome. Oh God, if only I could be banished."

"I told Papa the gossip was a lie."

Tears ran down Cornelia's cheeks.

"Papa said he wouldn't do anything if you'd go to your villa in the mountains for a year."

"They'll never let me go," Cornelia said dully. "Either of them."

Camilla shook Cornelia. "Listen to me. Here's what you can do."

Cornelia listened then said hopelessly, "I can't."

"Cornelia, you can. You must. It will work."

"But Titus will—"

"What will Titus do, my dear?" His deep voice cut across Cornelia's hoarse tone.

The sisters jerked around. Titus filled the doorway, blocking the sunlight. He walked heavily into the room, his head jutting forward. "Go ahead, Cornelia."

Camilla stood and faced him. "Cornelia is quite ill."

The words fell like stones into a well. Nothing moved in Titus's heavy, brooding face. He looked past Camilla. "Cornelia's never had a head for wine. She'll be all right."

The indifference in his voice angered Camilla, strengthened her. "She's burning up with fever," Camilla said firmly. "She must go to the mountains."

Titus's loose lips twisted in a sneer. He looked down at the bed. "The Emperor's waiting, Cornelia. Get up. Get your girls and fix yourself up." He half turned and started to clap his hands for the slaves.

"No." Camilla's voice was cold, decisive, implacable.

His heavy head turned and he looked at Camilla. His face flushed an ugly red. "Don't tell me what to do in my house."

"Your house. It's expensive to keep up, isn't it?"

He stared at her.

"You enjoy the income from Cornelia's villas, don't you?"

"What business is it of yours, Camilla?"

"I only want to make sure you don't lose that income."

Titus stepped toward her. "Lose it? How could I lose it?"

"My father intends to banish Cornelia if she doesn't leave Rome for a year. If he does, you'll be forced to divorce her and half her dowry will be returned to my father."

Titus grabbed Camilla's arm. "What are you talking about?" he demanded angrily.

She jerked free of his grip. "You went too far, Titus, when you gave Cornelia to the Emperor. My father knows and he's going to banish her if she doesn't leave Rome for a year with her sons and stay at the mountain villa with no guests at all."

"Caligula won't permit it." Titus's voice shook.

"He will if you convince him Cornelia has a fever. He hates sickness. You know that."

Camilla waited and prayed that Marcus was right about Caligula's squeamishness.

Titus began to pace up and down the bedroom like an angry bull. "I can't afford to make him angry."

"He'll thank you for protecting him from disease. Tell him you hurried her out of Rome as soon as you realized she was sick."

Titus stormed back and stared at her with hatred. "Damn you, Camilla, this is your fault. You've arranged it somehow."

"You brought it on yourself." If she hadn't despised him so much for the suffering and degradation he'd brought to Cornelia, Camilla would almost have felt sorry for him he was so obviously terrified of what Caligula might do if he was denied Cornelia. Pasty faced, his hands shaking, Titus muttered, "I'll go to the Palace now. He mustn't be disappointed. I'll find a girl. Someone special . . ."

As he hurried from the room, Camilla turned back to the bed. "Quickly, Cornelia. Call your litter bearers. Gather up the boys. Get on your way before he returns. I'll go see father."

Camilla left the household in disarray, slaves running frantically about, the litter-bearers gathering on the front steps.

As her litter stopped in front of her father's house, Camilla paused for a moment, then moved resolutely inside, trying to steady her thoughts. She must succeed. She found her father sitting in the darkened study, reclining on a couch with an unopened scroll in his lap. He looked up, his face somber. She knew he was weighing his decision, wondering whether he should stand firm to the principles he'd followed all his life.

Camilla hurried to his side. "I've talked to Cornelia. I want you to know she regrets with all her heart that she caused you pain." Camilla dropped down to her knees beside him and clasped his hands, such cold, hard hands. "Papa, she's broken-hearted. She's going to the mountain villa and she'll stay there for a year with the boys and no one will visit her. She and the boys will have a wonderful year. Papa, it will be all right."

"It was my daughter they talked about at the Baths," he said numbly. "I should denounce her."

Camilla gripped his hands tightly. "Papa, we agreed."

He began to shake his head.

"Papa, please. For my sake, for Cornelia's sake, let her leave with her boys. I promise you she'll stay at the villa."

His face softened as he looked at her. "You take care of all of us, don't you, Camilla?"

"I love Cornelia."

"I did love her," her father said emptily.

"Papa, she is so grieved. There are reasons."

"There is never a reason for immorality," he interrupted harshly. "If you are going to talk like that, I made a dreadful error in letting you become involved. Is the evil of one daughter going to eat away at the goodness of another daughter?"

"Cornelia is no more evil than I, Papa."

"You are never evil, my dear. I know that. I know that I can trust you. Always."

Camilla looked away. When Decimus divorced her, her father would be distraught. How would he feel when she married Marcus? If he ever had any inkling she and Marcus had been lovers, his anger—and grief—would be terrible.

She felt a terrible mingling of love and fear and sorrow and guilt. She said quietly, "I love you very much, Papa."

He rose and came to her and embraced her. Camilla embraced him in return, but she looked past him with troubled eyes.

"Sign here and here."

Camilla studied the wax tablet Decimus placed in front of her. The tablet contained an agreement whereby she promised the income from her Tuscany villa and from the Alban farms for two years. "Two years?"

"That gives me enough, Camilla."

She lifted the stylus then looked up at Decimus.

He leaned forward expectantly, his faun-like face taut and eager.

"When the trial is over, Decimus, you will divorce me in front of witnesses as you promised."

His mouth curved in a light smile. "I well understand, Camilla, that legal matters aren't binding unless written down or said in front of witnesses."

Satisfied, she bent forward and signed her name.

He grabbed up the tablet immediately. Then he paused. "Camilla, I wondered if we might talk it over."

"Talk what over?"

"A divorce. After all, we've gotten along quite well and you can be free to live as you wish."

She shook her head violently and the pleasant look slipped from his face.

"You've certainly developed a rather strong personality, Camilla. I don't envy your lover. Whoever he is."

She looked at him coldly. "You are welcome to whatever opinion you may hold of me, Decimus."

"You've blackmailed me," he said viciously, "and you've put

poor Titus into a real fix. How did you work that one? Did you tip your father so he'd go after Cornelia? You took a real chance there, Camilla."

Camilla looked down at her estate books, ignoring him.

"I wonder what your father would do if he knew you have a lover?" Decimus mused.

She looked up, startled.

He laughed, "So I can still get your attention. But it's all right, Camilla. It wouldn't suit my purposes to have you banished."

"I signed the money over to you," she reminded him.

"So I'm to remember I'm being paid and not cause any trouble." His tone was harsh.

Camilla stared at him.

He shrugged. "All right. We made a deal." His face hardened. "But I don't like a woman telling me what to do." He turned and left the study.

Camilla watched him go. Long after his footsteps faded away, she went over and over the conversation in her mind. Decimus was more dangerous and angry than she realized. But she had his word.

Now only the trial stood between her and her freedom. The trial began tomorrow.

XIV

Camilla was up at first light. She knew Decimus must be awake, too. The house was subdued, the slaves moving about very quietly. They, too, would be worried, knowing that the day's outcome would affect their lives as did everything that happened to their master. They would wonder, perhaps, that she and Decimus didn't talk this morning, but they must have wondered many times about their master and mistress.

Camilla dressed in a sober gray gown. The Senate was closed to women, of course, but Marcus wanted her to wait in the hallway outside the senate chamber so the senators would see her as they entered. Decimus's brothers and Terentia's husband would be in the Senate chamber. Terentia would join her in the hallway. Word had already spread over Rome about Cornelia's illness and her hasty departure for her mountain villa because her Greek doctor prescribed the cool air to quiet her fever. Camilla's father would sit with Decimus and his kinsmen. Family solidarity was important, Marcus stressed. It could mean the difference between conviction and acquittal.

The trial began at the third hour in the Curia of Julius Caesar. Almost all of the 300 seats were filled. The trial of a senator by his peers didn't happen often.

Decimus and his family members took their seats on the front row to the left. From her vantage point outside, Camilla could see her father's beaked profile. He looked stern and serious.

The presiding consul took his place on the dais. Lesser magistrates sat on either side. The consul lit the sacred fire in a bowl before the robed figure of Libertas, the goddess of freedom. Several priests moved ceremoniously in front of the dais and lifted a caged bird for all to see. Several pieces of grain were dropped into his cage. Everyone strained to see. The bird, denied food for two days, gobbled down the grain. The senators relaxed. The auspices were good. The trial could begin.

The prosecutor, Lucius Jucundus, strode dramatically to the open space before the dais. He waited until all quieted and looked toward him. His ascetic face intense, he began.

"I bring before members of this venerable body information of a disgrace so sickening, a corruption so repugnant, that your hearts will burn with anger and dismay. You will rise up to shout that this corruptor must be punished." He paused and leaned forward. "It is your duty to vote death to Decimus Rufini."

The evidence, of course, had already been presented to the judge who sat on the dais. His morning would be devoted to arguments for conviction by the prosecutor and for acquittal by Marcus. Decimus's fate would be decided by a vote of all the senators.

A water clock trickled away the time. Camilla stood outside the open door to the chamber and listened with increasing concern to Jucundus's virulent accusations. He raised his arms to implore the heavens. Camilla felt faint as the catalogue of criminal acts by Decimus grew, mounting like a stinking heap of fish offal.

Sympathetic observers near the exit looked at her curiously.

Camilla tried not to show her distress, but the disclosures appalled her. None surprised her. There was little she would put past Decimus, but the stories of his obscene cruelties to house slaves attached to the official residence made her wonder that she could have shared a home, however distantly, with a man for so many years without the least indication of this kind of depravity. But she knew of other depravity.

As Jucundus swept to his climax, Camilla felt a wave of panic. The accusations were much worse than she had imagined. No wonder Marcus had diverted her inquiries. How could Marcus hope to persuade the senators to vote for Decimus? The story was too grim, the transgressions too vividly depicted. The gods were against them today.

Jucundus closed with a mighty shout. "Death to Decimus Rufini."

Camilla felt a rush of pride as Marcus stood and walked toward the front. He looked calm, confident, unworried. He wore his toga elegantly, as if it had no weight. The toga hung in perfect folds and shone with crisp, brilliant whiteness. Marcus's thick, curly black hair glistened in a shaft of sunlight that speared through a high window, framing him in a golden circle of light. He looked honorable and strong. He bowed to the judges, then faced the rows of senators with a confident smile.

Camilla felt despair. No matter how superbly he spoke, how could Marcus possibly save Decimus? If Marcus failed, they could never marry because people would whisper that he had deliberately lost the case to get rid of Decimus. Camilla clenched her hands. No wonder Marcus was worried those last days at the shore. It took all Camilla's strength to stand and watch as Marcus spoke, because she foresaw the end of all their hopes. How unfair it was that her future should rest on Decimus's fate. Would she never be free of him?

"Rome honors Romans," Marcus said quietly, his tone even and dignified, in studied contrast to Jucundus's strident oration.

"We have in this chamber today many honorable Romans. It is a great honor to recognize today one of Rome's heroes."

Marcus paused and the senators rustled in their seats, certain he couldn't be referring to Decimus, yet puzzled at this beginning.

"It would be nice if this were a happier occasion for Senator Publius Cornelius Scipio. But he is here, after a lapse of years, to show support for his son-in-law, Decimus Claudius Rufini.

"I want all of us to remember today the kind of Romans we admire, the kind of Roman that is Publius Cornelius Scipio." Marcus described in detail her father's impressive career, his Army duty, his golden oratory, his governorship of Gaul. Senator Scipio's old friends nodded among themselves. Younger senators craned to see him.

"Publius Scipio has no sons. If he had, they would follow his lead, seeking to serve Rome as best they could. Senator Scipio does have a son-in-law."

Voices murmured and there was an angry, threatening undertone.

Marcus continued quickly, "It would be hard for any man to follow in the footsteps of Publius Scipio. Decimus Rufini makes no claim such as that, but he has compiled an honorable record."

Whistles and hisses sounded.

Marcus ignored the sounds, but Camilla tensed. Wasn't Marcus off on the wrong track? Almost anyone's career would pale in comparison with her father's, but especially Decimus's. The contrast was too great.

Marcus spoke loudly to be heard. "The evidence against Decimus Rufini is great. Senator Rufini himself now feels that in his eagerness to increase the taxable receipts for the benefit of the Empire and to the glory of the Emperor, he did indeed go too far in pressing the people for money. In his defense, let us be clear:

"He built more roads than any governor in the last thirty years.

"He directed the construction of a new amphitheatre which will hold fifty thousand spectators and dedicated it to the memory of Augustus.

"He maintained complete control of Syria."

Marcus paused, said emphatically, "These things he did well. What do his accusers say? They claim he ordered the torture of slaves attached to the official mansion. Do these accusers tell you why he ordered their torture?" Marcus looked hard at the listening senators. "They do not tell you that he suspected a conspiracy against the life of the Emperor!"

A tide of voices rose.

Marcus leaned forward and pounded his fist in his palm. "What must a governor of a province do when he suspects conspiracy? He—must—root—it—out!"

The senators shouted in agreement.

Marcus held up his hands. "This is what Decimus Rufini did for the glory of the Empire and the protection of the Emperor. Everyone knows that the testimony of any slave is suspect and can only be tested under torture."

Heads nodded in agreement. An old senator in the front row said loudly, "That's the truth, my lad, that's the truth."

"Decimus Rufini did his duty as he saw it," Marcus continued. "Today, he wishes me to tell his fellow senators, many of whom have served hard terms in the provinces and know of its difficulties, that this morning he delivered to the Senate a sum of money equal in amount to the sum he is accused of taking from the people of Syria."

A wave of approbation swept the Curia.

"I ask you, as we come to this vote, to recall the heroes Decimus Rufini has followed. Foremost, of course, he gives honor to the

Emperor. He gives honor to his fellow senators. Finally, he carries with him, always, his regard for that most honorable of Romans, his father-in-law, Senator Publius Cornelius Scipio."

Cheers broke out.

"Vote today as you would wish to be voted for. Remember, Decimus Rufini is one of you."

As many of the senators cheered, Marcus gave a short bow and joined Decimus. Camilla's father clapped him on the shoulder, but Decimus gave him a curiously bloodless look and a short nod.

Marcus, flushed with exertion, looked alive and vital and commanding. Camilla realized then how much it meant to him to be an orator. This was where he belonged, here or in the courts, scrapping, struggling, battling to win. He had told her that nothing mattered so much to him as she. But a man must have his sphere of greatness. She must never do anything to jeopardize his career.

If he lost today, it wouldn't ruin his career unless he then married her. If he did, the conclusion in Rome would be inescapable that he had taken a case to be sure of gaining her freedom.

Marcus looked toward the exit.

She framed the words, "You were wonderful."

He looked relieved and pleased, then turned away as others bent to congratulate him.

Fear and hope battled within her. The accusations against Decimus seemed insurmountable, but Marcus had argued skillfully and drawn beautifully upon the senators' regard for her father.

What would the vote be? Freedom? Or death?

A nerve throbbed in her neck. She clasped her hands as discussion began.

Senator Serenus, a former consul and the oldest member present, stood to speak. Gradually silence fell. Senator Serenus leaned on his walking stick. "Senator Rufini's advocate is well spoken," he said in his thin old man's voice.

Applause erupted.

"I understand this young man is newly returned from studies in Greece and has enjoyed a rapid success in his first cases." The old man paused. "Perhaps our young orator should return to Greece for further studies."

Togas rustled and several senators hissed their disapproval.

A small smile touched Serenus's grim mouth. His dark, hooded eyes slowly surveyed his peers. "Ah, there is a wave of support for our young advocate." He nodded judiciously. "Yes, young Marcus Julius Paulus spoke well. Many believe him to be one of the most promising orators to grace our halls since Cicero." Again, he nodded. "I, too, believe this young man's future will shine like gold. But, as senators of Rome," and his voice strengthened, "we should not be dazzled by graceful words and artful phrases. Instead, we should strike to the heart of the argument as a Roman soldier strikes to the heart of his foe."

"Hear, hear!" a senator shouted.

Senator Serenus nodded to himself several times. "When we strike to the heart of our young orator's argument, why, we find nothing there. His words are empty. They are clever and forceful and persuasive, but empty. My fellow senators, we are not here today to recall the glories of Rome or the accomplishments of our most revered Senator Publius Cornelius Scipio; we are here to determine the guilt or innocence of Decimus Rufini." He stamped his ebony black cane against the marble floor. "Decimus Rufini is guilty!"

"Guilty!" a senator shouted from the back row. Others joined him. "Guilty! Guilty!"

Camilla knew many of those shouting for Decimus's death. She'd shared meals with them in her father's house.

"Guilty of what?" a deep voiced demanded. Cornelia's husband, Titus, bullnecked and powerful, stood up and a sudden hush fell. Titus's thick lips parted in a slight smile. He knew his power as a favorite of the Emperor. Titus looked up and down the rows, seeking out the eyes of men he knew.

Their glances fell away.

"It is time indeed for thought," Titus rasped. "The Emperor hears whispers of conspiracy. He knows there are enemies."

His words hung in the tense room. Faces smoothed themselves empty of expression. No one looked at his neighbor. The senators scarcely breathed.

If Caligula decided that a senator wished him ill, it took only a word and a man must open his veins. It was cold and still now in the Curia.

Titus nodded slowly. "That's right, my fellow senators. Think. What did Decimus Rufini do?" His voice boomed. "He saved our Emperor. Do we curse him for that? Do we order him to his death for defending his Emperor?"

Colder still. Senators shrank in their seats, shoulders hunched, eyes averted.

Titus punched his right fist into the air. "Let's vote. Let's vote now!"

Slowly, the shouts came. "Vote!" "Vote now!" "For the Emperor!" The senators stood and the shouts turned into a roar. "Acquit him!" "He's innocent!" "He saved the Emperor!"

When the vote was over, senators crowded around Decimus, congratulating him, clapping him on the shoulder. They moved in a swirl of togas and noise out into the immense hall and her father held up his hands for quiet. "Everyone come to my home and we will celebrate our success. We will rejoice at the acquittal of a good servant of Rome and we will celebrate the triumph of an outstanding advocate. We will give thanks, too, for the bonds of friendship and family loyalty," and he held out his hand to Titus.

Camilla watched, sickened. If her father knew only a portion of the truth about Titus, he would never touch him. As for the real reason for Titus championing Decimus, she had an idea of why he'd come as Decimus's champion. She'd often wondered at the close relationship between Decimus and Titus. When she saw the glance that passed between the two men, she knew her insight was true. A shudder of revulsion swept her.

"Camilla, are you all right?" Terentia looked at her anxiously.

"Yes. I'm just upset."

"I know, you must have been terrified." Terentia said sympathetically. "Camilla, I'm so happy for you." Then she said shyly, "I'll bet you and Decimus wish you could be alone, but we have to go to Papa's, don't we?"

Camilla started to tell Terentia the truth, but resisted. It wasn't time yet. Not until she was divorced. Freedom was near now. Surely her father couldn't be angry if Decimus initiated the divorce. She and Marcus would wait for a while. She hated to delay their wedding by even a day, but she must give thought to her father's feelings.

She tried to form her face into a welcome for Decimus and thought that soon she would no longer have to pretend.

Decimus, flushed with triumph, called out, "Camilla."

She managed a smile.

He came up to her and slipped his arm around her shoulders. She stiffened warily.

"My good wife," he called out, and his voice carried in the echoing hallway. The he bent and his mouth touched hers.

Shocked, Camilla started to twist away, but his arm held her tightly and his mouth pressed roughly against hers. It seemed an age of indignity before he lifted his head. His dark eyes glittering with malice, he said, loudly again, “My good wife. Now we go to celebrate.”

Marcus stood a few feet away, his face turned to stone and then she lost sight of him as senators surrounded him.

Angry red spots burned on Camilla’s cheeks as she climbed into the litter. She almost directed her litterearers to turn homeward. However, her father would never understand if she didn’t come. Why should she go to her father’s to celebrate for Decimus? Wasn’t this more of the lie that was going to end soon?

She gave a decisive nod. They wanted to celebrate. She would celebrate. Marcus’s triumph marked the end of her marriage. She would go to the celebration and she would talk to Marcus. If other eyes watched, who cared now?

She was smiling by the time she hurried into her father’s reception hall. In the crush of arrivals, she caught Marcus’s eye.

He nodded.

Camilla slipped out to the garden first. She waited by the central fountain. When Marcus walked down the marble steps, she felt her heart would burst from joy.

They met midway along the path.

“Marcus, you were wonderful, absolutely wonderful.”

“Thank you, Camilla.” But his face folded in a frown. “Why did Decimus kiss you?”

“He’s angry. But let him be angry.” Standing in the sunlight with Marcus, she hardly cared now about Decimus’s unwanted touch. “Soon he can’t cause us any unhappiness. Don’t think about him. Think about your triumph today. No one could have done better.”

They walked down a thick avenue of fir trees and found a quiet pocket. She slipped into his arms.

Marcus nuzzled his face against her cheek. “Let’s go to my apartment.”

Camilla hesitated. Would they be missed? Then, eagerly, defiantly, she said, "I will meet you there."

They separated in the courtyard and each entered the reception hall alone. The huge room echoed with the boom of men's loud voices. Although it was still early afternoon, several senators had already had too much to drink. She glimpsed her father standing near the masks of his ancestors, his own face masklike. He disliked drinking bouts.

Camilla struggled through a throng of ebullient senators. One of them clapped her on the back shouting, "Here's Decimus's lady. We all know there will be a real celebration tonight." The men broke into raucous laughter.

Camilla's father glared at them.

Camilla threaded her way to her father. "I'm going home now," she said loudly over the din.

Her father nodded. "Yes, you should."

She touched his arm. "I'll talk to you soon."

As she left the reception hall, she saw Titus, his face flushed and his arm draped heavily over Decimus's shoulders.

Camilla wondered if any of the senators saw what she saw. But perhaps this was more common among men than she knew. Perhaps it would surprise no one. She'd been thankful before that Decimus never made love to her because of the boys. To think that he and Titus—but she wouldn't think about them together, she wouldn't picture what they did. Their actions could have no effect on her now.

She climbed into her litter with a sense of freedom. Though, as she jolted toward Marcus' apartment, she worried about her father's reaction to her divorce. Would he be angry? She hoped not. Loving Marcus was more important to her than anything else, including her father.

Marcus came first.

She hurried through Aristides's shop and up the stairs to Marcus's apartment. He opened the door, and she flew into his arms. He swung her up in the air and whirled her around before setting her down.

"Camilla, we're going to be together," he said happily.

"You've won my freedom."

"It took more than my defense of Decimus. You were brave enough to face him down and demand your freedom in exchange for the money. That took courage." He smoothed Camilla's hair, lightly touched her cheek. "I can't believe that we're going to finally be together—forever."

"It's true." Camilla felt almost dizzy with joy. She cupped his face in her hands. "I love you more than anything or anyone in the whole world."

"Do you?" he teased. "Can you prove how much you love me?"

"I think I can," she said softly. "Let's try and see."

She stood on tiptoe and covered his face with small kisses, each as light and quick as airborne down. Slowly her lips lingered and her tongue touched the corner of his mouth, edged ever so delicately between his lips.

Marcus's mouth covered hers and desire burned between them hot and fiery as a flame.

Camilla pulled away long enough to gasp, "You didn't give me time to show you . . ."

"I can't wait," he said urgently and his hands tugged at her gown. They moved in a flurry then, shedding his stiff toga and her lighter gown. Marcus swept her up in his arms to carry her to his room. They tumbled onto the bed, scarcely aware of their surroundings, moving eagerly together, plunging in a whirling ecstasy that defied time and thought. Only feeling and sensation existed in the small, immense world created by the two of them.

"Marcus, Marcus, Marcus," she moaned.

Finally, they lay quietly, their faces close together, looking into each other's eyes.

Marcus smiled. "Every day you are more beautiful."

"Do you suppose we'll ever tire of this?" she asked sleepily.

He propped up on an elbow and looked down at her, his eyes dancing. "Absolutely not. I promise."

She ran her hand up his arm. "When we marry, could you take time off from the courts so we can go to Swallow's Nest?"

"I may take off forever."

"You're too good an orator ever to quit. But for a week or so."

"At least for a week or so. We'll make love at first light and as the sun sets. . . ."

"And every afternoon."

"Love in the afternoon. That will always be best of all."

They held hands and talked softly, planning their tomorrows, pausing sometimes to kiss and caress but, soon, too soon, the afternoon sun slanted high on the eastern wall.

As Camilla dressed, she said happily, "This will be the last time I ever have to leave you, Marcus. I'm going to ask Decimus to divorce me as soon as I get home."

When she reached home, though the sun hung in the west, Decimus wasn't there. Camilla ate dinner, then walked in the courtyard. It was, as always, very beautiful but she knew she wouldn't miss it. It didn't matter to her. Nor did the huge opulent home matter. Decimus could have it all, though, of course, half her property would be returned to her. When she told her father of the divorce, she would suggest they permit Decimus to keep this house. She knew how much he valued expensive properties.

She walked until night fell, then shrugged and turned toward her room. Decimus was so late now that he was probably drunk. She'd talk to him in the morning. That would be a good time because the divorce must be witnessed, and morning would see the steady arrival of lesser citizens who depended upon Decimus for support and funds. Morning would do very well indeed.

It was late in the night when she heard Decimus arrive, shouting in a thick voice as he stumbled through the reception hall. Another, deeper voice answered. So Titus had come home with him. Long after the noise of their arrival subsided, Camilla lay sleepless, but she didn't think about her husband or his lover. She thought of Marcus and the years of happiness they were going to share.

She woke at first light and dressed swiftly. When her morning slave hurried in with a basin of warm water, Camilla washed her face then said, "Go quickly and see if the master is awake. Let me know as soon as he arises."

Camilla paced up and down in the courtyard, a shawl draped over her shoulders to ward off the chilly autumn air.

Soon, soon, soon. Only minutes now. What should she do first? Her slaves would gather up all of her belongings. She'd move home to her father's house. If all went well, he'd welcome her. Marcus would come to call and one day soon, perhaps during the Saturnalia, they would wed.

"Mistress, the master's in the study."

Camilla hurried inside. It was still gray in the house. Wax lamps glimmered in the study where Decimus reclined on a couch, studying a scroll.

He looked up as she entered. "I missed you at the party yesterday afternoon."

She ignored his questioning statement. "Decimus, you can divorce me this morning. As soon as some of your clients come."

He made no response.

"They can be the witnesses."

"Witnesses?"

"You know," she said impatiently. "You have to divorce me in front of witnesses. How many is it?"

Decimus looked back down at the scroll. "Seven, I believe."

"You'll certainly have that many clients."

Decimus re-rolled the scroll. "I've been looking at the financial reports on your villas. It looks like profits will be up considerably."

"What does it matter?"

He shook his head.

Camilla frowned. "What do you mean?"

He tilted his head to look up at her and she was struck once again by the feline curve of his mouth, the heavy pouches beneath his eyes, his general air of seediness and dissolution. He began to smile. "It's very simple, Camilla. There isn't going to be a divorce."

Camilla clutched the tall metal lampstand for support. She felt dizzy and shaken, as if the earth had heaved beneath her feet. But the room lay unchanged, cool and gray and dim, filled with busts of poets and tall wooden racks holding hundreds of scrolls. A restful, repose-filled room until now.

"Decimus . . ." Her voice sounded thin and insubstantial.

He picked up another scroll.

"Decimus, look at me." Anger hardened her voice.

"Do sit down, Camilla. Stop shouting."

She reached out and swept the pile of scrolls from the table. They clattered to the floor. "You promised me."

He laughed, a tone of genuine amusement in his voice. "Really, Camilla, did I?"

"Decimus, I gave you the money."

"A wife's duty, my dear. Now I've been exonerated. Really, your young man did a lovely job." He looked up at her, his dark eyes gleaming with malice.

Camilla drew her breath in sharply.

The amusement seeped out of his face, leaving it flat and hostile. "Did you think me an absolute fool, Camilla?"

He'd known all the while about Marcus. It would be Priscus, of course. Priscus and his spying eyes.

Camilla lifted her chin. "I didn't think about you at all."

Decimus shrugged. "Fair enough. I don't spend any time in bed thinking about you."

Their hatred lay out in the open now, quivering like a live thing.

"Decimus," she tried to speak evenly, dispassionately, "we don't care about each other. That's true. Now is our chance to be free of each other to do as we wish. You can buy as many boys as you wish."

Once again, he shook his head.

"Decimus, you promised to free me. You promised if I gave you the money."

"I don't remember that at all," he said softly. Once again his mouth curved in a sly smile. "You'll recall, Camilla, we talked once about how there have to be witnesses to make a contract legal. You don't have any witnesses."

"Decimus, please." She hated to beg him, hated it, but she'd thought this would be the first day of freedom, the first day to plan a life filled with love. "Marcus saved you," she pled. "He made a wonderful argument."

"He did all right. But the senators voted for me because of Titus. Good old Titus. He's the one who saved me."

"If you divorce me, I'll ask Papa to let you keep this house and half of my dowry. That's enough for you. That's a lot of money."

He narrowed his eyes in thought. Camilla leaned forward anxiously.

Once again, he shook his head and she realized he'd been toying with her, encouraging her to plead for his own pleasure.

"Sorry, Camilla, but you're too useful to me."

"Useful?"

He looked at her in mock surprise. "You amaze me. I suppose it's true that love blinds. Did you really think I'd divorce you and lose my link to your family and my use of your income? I'd have to be crazy."

"You promised."

"I don't remember that," he said in a bored voice. He laughed again. "Besides, if I divorced you all the Roman mamas would be after me to marry their bucktoothed daughters and it would be so tiring to evade them. Why don't you relax. Perhaps you'd like to go back to Swallow's Nest."

She stared at him with a kind of sick fascination. Now she knew the depths of his dishonesty and cruelty.

"Don't look so forlorn," he said lightly. "I don't mind if you have a lover. Have several."

Her face turned deathly pale. "I only want Marcus. I want to be his wife."

"That you'll never be," he said roughly.

Anger swept her. She could see the years passing and herself forever chained to this man who didn't love her, forced to live with a man who loved little boys and her own brother-in-law.

"I hate you," she said raggedly.

He quirked an eyebrow. "Do you? That's too bad, Camilla. So wearing for you. Really, we can have a very nice arrangement. You may take your lover with you wherever you go. I won't tell your father so long as you share your income without a quarrel. I dislike quarrels, you know."

"I will bear Marcus's child," she said furiously.

"That's all right." His sensual mouth curved in a smile. "After all, the child might be a little boy. If so, you know how much I'll enjoy him."

XV

"Don't despair," Marcus said softly.

She lifted a tear-streaked face. "How can I do otherwise?"

Marcus jammed blunt fingers through his thick hair. "There has to be a way."

Slowly, wearily, Camilla shook her head. "We're trapped, Marcus. I'll never be free. Never."

"Damn him," Marcus swore, his voice low and hard. He grimaced and began to pace.

Camilla watched hopelessly.

Marcus stopped and pulled her to her feet. "Camilla, we'll run away." The muscles in his jaw were taut, his eyes wild.

This was a Marcus she'd never seen, a man enraged beyond caution.

She knew the answer. "We can't. You know that. They'd find us."

He didn't answer because he knew the truth of it. They'd be found. The rule of Rome stretched over the world to the farthest desert and ocean outposts. They'd be found. The Emperor could order death to those convicted of adultery or order their banishment to distant hellholes and confiscate their estates. Caligula enjoyed confiscating estates.

"I don't care," Marcus retorted.

Camilla shook her head. "We're trapped. There's nothing we can do."

Marcus stared at her, his face rigid. She wondered if, through his fury, he saw her at all. His face softened. "Don't look like that, Camilla. Don't be frightened."

"I am frightened. I can't bear it if you do something mad for me and ruin your life. We must stay here. I don't want you hurt. Not ever. Never because of me."

His hands gently cupped her face. "Sometimes love has to be painful," he said, almost to himself. He bent down and lightly kissed her. "The love we've had is surely worth all the pain in the world. I would run away with you—"

"No," she said again.

"—but I don't want to lose you. We can still love each other."

Camilla looked away. "At Decimus's pleasure," she said bitterly.

"Yes," he said heavily. "There's that."

They didn't talk about that ugly truth. Their future, what love they shared, would be at Decimus's whim with his ever-present threat to inform her father.

"He won't tell Papa, because he wants my money," she said grimly.

"Perhaps someday . . ." Marcus said quietly.

"Perhaps . . ."

Tears welled again in Camilla's eyes.

"Don't cry," he said gently. "We love each other. No matter what happens, we have that. Not Decimus nor your father nor the Emperor can ruin that."

She managed a tremulous smile and looked up at him, at his dear face with the bright dark eyes and bold nose and blunt chin. He was right. Nothing could destroy the love they'd known, but she wanted more than stolen hours now. She'd looked ahead to a long life with Marcus as his wife, encouraging him, loving him, bearing his children.

Now that dream had ended.

Marcus grieved, too. She saw the sadness in his eyes, in the tired droop of his shoulders. His pain intensified her pain. She reached out and they came into each other's arms. She felt the beating of his heart and she ached with love and caring. She buried her face against his neck. Gently, Marcus picked her up and carried her to his room.

To make love, she thought soberly, in all seasons and for all reasons, in joy and sorrow, on good days and bad, because they cared. They undressed slowly and lay together on the narrow bed, the coverlet drawn up to their shoulders to ward away the October chill. Camilla gently caressed his cheek, then lightly kissed his lips. Quietly and softly as snowflakes slip against a leaden sky, they touched and talked. Then the magic began, the fiery, magnificent explosion of passion. They kissed almost desperately and came together in a glorious union as wild and violent as storm-driven waves crashing to shore.

Then Camilla lay quietly in his arms and smiled into his eyes.

"No tears now," he said.

"No tears."

Marcus slipped his hand through her long black hair. "We're still the lucky ones, Camilla, you and I."

"I know."

"We won't ever give up," he said determinedly, and she knew he was telling her that they would be together no matter what and that this love was enough for him, even if all they ever had were hours such as these.

Camilla rested her face against his chest. She didn't answer. Someday she knew she must look to the future and do what was best for Marcus because she loved him. For now, at least for the next weeks and months, surely it would be fair enough before the gods if she clung to his love.

She wouldn't count on forever.

"Camilla," he said sharply.

He knew, of course. He always knew her thoughts.

"Camilla, look at me."

She lifted her face. "I love you," she said simply.

"You're all I want from life." His words were forceful.

"I love you," she said again.

"Don't break my heart," he whispered, and she saw the shine of tears in his eyes.

She pulled his face down to hers.

She carried the memory of the sad, soft warmth of his tears as she rode homeward in her litter. Deep in her heart she knew that someday, one day, she would send him away. Her heart would break and life would hold no promise or joy, but Marcus must have a wife and a family. She couldn't give him that.

If she had a child, Marcus would know it to be his. Camilla felt a thrill of happiness. Perhaps, after all . . . She shuddered. If she had a son would Decimus molest him? She knew the answer, knew with sick certainty. Camilla slumped in her litter. She didn't dare conceive. If she bore a son and Decimus touched him, Camilla knew she would destroy Decimus no matter what the cost.

When the litter stopped in front of her house, it took Camilla a long moment to force herself to alight. She didn't want to see Decimus. Not today. Not any day, of course. But especially not today.

Her mouth set, she walked inside. This was, after all, her house. If Decimus wanted the use of her money and her family name, she would extract cooperation from him, more than the tacit understanding that she would see Marcus. From now on, she and Decimus wouldn't share meals. She wanted to see as little of him as possible. She wasn't going to let him trample on her. She was trapped, but she was going to fight.

She was prepared for battle when she saw Priscus.

"I want to see your master," she said shortly.

Priscus nodded deferentially, but his eyes were knowing and arrogant.

Camilla felt sure it was Priscus who'd followed her and told Decimus about Marcus.

"I'm sorry, Mistress, the master isn't here. He left word to tell you he would be out of town for several days."

Priscus didn't say where Decimus had gone. Camilla didn't ask. She merely nodded and turned away, but felt a distinct lightening of her mood.

Camilla ate dinner alone in the courtyard and felt lonely. Marcus would be eating now, too. His apartment was only twenty minutes by litter, but it might as well be in Spain or Gaul. Camilla toyed with her food, succulent lamb covered with a sweet date sauce and fried carrots and creamed squash. She ate only a bite or two, shook her head, and a slave carried the servings away. He returned with dessert, cheese balls deep fried in olive oil, soaked in honey and sprinkled with poppy seeds. Camilla ate one.

When her hands were washed, she slipped on her sandals and walked restlessly in the garden. Calling for her cloak, she walked briskly past the splashing fountains to the iron gate that opened into the parkland. It was already twilight, the early dusk of fall. She hurried up the twisting path, slipping a little on the pine needles in her eagerness. She paused to look with smiling eyes at the arbor where she and Marcus had spoken of love. Marcus had asked her to come the next day to his apartment. She'd had girlish fancies of love mixed with the sometimes bitter, sometimes lustful descriptions of her friends. Now she knew what it was to love a man, to hold him within her and share the flood of passion that walls away the world. Happy with her memories, Camilla climbed up the hill to the summerhouse with its glorious view of home. She stared down at the city, watching dusk envelop the marble temples and tufa-faced apartments.

"Mistress." The call came softly as a dove's coo.

Startled, Camilla turned. She stiffened.

The boys crouched only a few feet from her, the whites of their eyes glittering in the twilight.

"Yes," she said shortly.

One of the twins stepped closer.

"Mistress," he whispered, "the master's gone to Ostia."

She heard fear in his voice and abruptly she understood. "He didn't take you."

The boy shook his head. His mouth quivered. "He took the yellow boys."

Camilla nodded. So Decimus was enamored of his new boys, the golden-haired twins from Germany.

"Do you mind so much?" she asked gently.

The boys' eyes slid away from hers. "He's talking about selling us."

The unknown evil, of course, was much more fearsome than the known. Camilla bit her lip. Didn't Decimus care at all for them as children? She knew the answer. Decimus cared only for feelings and pleasure and these children were instruments. What could she do? Perhaps she could talk to her father, ask him to buy them from Decimus. Then the boys would be safe.

"I'll try to help," she said quietly. "I don't know if I can, but I'll try."

The second twin edged nearer. "You made us well."

She shrugged. "I called the doctor when you were sick. He made you well."

"You called him," he persisted, "even though you didn't like us."

Such a clear, straight judgment he made. Camilla's heart ached. They were only children yet they'd known how she hated seeing them.

"It wasn't you," she said haltingly. "It was him."

The first twin, she thought him to be Alexander, stepped closer. He looked back over his shoulder. Ajax looked back, too. Tension tightened the muscles in their necks, made their pointed faces even sharper. Alexander finished his careful scrutiny of the path and the thick-limbed trees that crowded close to the summerhouse. Motioning to his brother, they scurried up the steps and hunkered down beneath the waist high railing. Now they were hidden from view outside the summerhouse.

Camilla looked down at them, puzzled and just a little frightened.

"Please, Mistress," Ajax whispered, "Look out at the city. If anyone comes up the path, he will think you are alone."

Slowly, Camilla looked out across the darkening city. Flares flickered outside the Emperor's Palace. A banquet must be in progress. "What is it, Ajax?"

Somehow, she knew before he spoke that his words would change her life. It was the stealthy way they'd crept to see her and the fear that made their young faces look old.

Alexander leaned forward. He spoke in a whisper, but Camilla heard every word. "Slaves know things."

Camilla nodded. Yes, slaves knew things, knew their masters' loves and hates, their fears and terrible dark yearnings and hidden passions. Oh yes, slaves knew things.

"The master's gone to Ostia to pick up a new slave."

What did that matter to her, Camilla wondered. Let Decimus buy all the boys he wanted. It sickened her, but she no longer cared.

Alexander plucked at her gown. "This slave costs much money. They say he's from a northern place and he carries a satchel of dark leather and no one dares look within it."

Something in the tone of his high little voice made her back prickle.

"A satchel?" Her gaze slid down to look at the crouched boys.

Alexander nodded, and Ajax, too.

They spoke together and their combined whispers sounded like the eerie wind that tugs and pulls at roof tiles.

"Poisons. He carries poisons."

Camilla drew her breath in sharply. Air knotted in her lungs. She reached out and clung to the railing for support. She looked down at the crouching twins. Their eyes gleamed, huge and frightened.

"Why does he carry poisons?" she asked, her voice now as high and thin as theirs.

Once again, their narrow heads turned together and they looked around the summerhouse and up and down the path, straining to see in the growing gloom. Together, they turned back to Camilla.

"He wants . . ." Ajax whispered.

". . . to kill you," Alexander completed.

Camilla lay rigid in her bed. Every so often a shudder swept her. How hideous to be poisoned. To eat or drink, never suspecting, then to have the bile surge in your throat and fiery, agonizing pain stab inside you.

She watched shifting shadows on the wall. She pictured Decimus's face, his jaded eyes and flaccid cheeks. Decimus didn't intend to take any chance of losing her dowry. If she died, he would inherit everything. He'd never have to ask for money again. So much money. It could buy fresh young twins every year and expensive statues and fine furniture and paintings. The farms and the villa at the shore would all belong to Decimus and no woman would be telling him what he could or couldn't do with any of it.

Camilla pressed her hands against her cheeks. Priscus had said he'd be gone for several days. So she had a day or two.

Camilla pushed back her covers and rose and paced up and down. She knew her way in the dark. But now she faced a dark and perilous path that led to danger and death.

One route to safety was absolutely barred. She couldn't tell Marcus. Marcus would kill Decimus. Camilla knew that very simply, knew it as well as she knew the feel of her own heartbeat. She could never tell Marcus, because he would kill Decimus and then he would be executed.

She could tell her father.

Camilla crossed to her door, opened it and looked out into the moonlight-silvered courtyard. She slipped quietly across the pavement to a stone bench beside the central fountain. Water splashed gently down into the pool, a soft and soothing sound in the night. She couldn't see the water. It was only a darker darkness in the night. But she knew it was there, clean and clear. It reminded her of Marcus and the dark cold water off the bluff and the strength of his arms and the utter sense of safety when he held her.

She couldn't tell Marcus.

She sat, cold and chilled, and watched the slow spread of dawn, the tiny quivering fingers of pink that edged into the dark gray horizon, the spreading patches of gold and orange and, finally, the brilliant sweep of the dawn.

Camilla dressed and called for her litter. It was just past the first hour. Her father would be receiving his clients. She didn't want to stay another instant in this house.

A cluster of slaves waited outside her father's house. They belonged to the visiting clients. Camilla walked into the reception hall. A swirl of togas made way for her.

"Good morning, Miss Camilla," called out Gallio, an old client she remembered from childhood. "How nice to see your pretty face this morning."

She managed a smile. "Thank you. It's good to see you again, too."

Her father, his eyes surprised, saw her through the crowd.

"Good morning, Camilla. Is something wrong?"

She nodded. "I must talk to you, but finish with your clients. I'll wait in the courtyard."

"I won't be long," her father said quickly.

Camilla walked slowly through the house. It seemed long ago and far away that this had been home. She had no sense of belonging. Or safety.

In the courtyard, she lifted her eyes to follow the line of thin poplars along the wall. She'd loved those trees as a child, spent hours watching their slender limbs bend in the wind, wondering what if felt like to be a leaf high in the air with the warmth of the sun pressing down. In the fall she grieved when the wind swept the leaves away, flinging them to the ground. Was she to be as helpless as a leaf?

Camilla pressed her hands against her mouth. She heard the scrape of a shoe on the pavement and turned.

"Camilla, my dear, what's wrong?" her father asked anxiously. He came up with a worried frown. "Has something happened to Decimus?"

She looked up at him, her eyes full of sorrow and anguish. "Papa, you must help me."

"Of course, I'll help you. You know that. Tell me what's upsetting you."

She didn't soften her message. She blurted the words out. "Decimus is going to kill me." Her voice rose and she reached out.

Her father stood very still. His arm went rigid under her hand. He stared, his face shocked—and disbelieving. "Camilla, you must not be well."

Her mouth twisted in mirthless laughter. "Not well. You are right, you know. I will be very, very sick—sick to death—if Decimus has his way."

Her father drew himself up, looked at her sternly. "You aren't yourself."

"Oh yes, Papa. I am myself. I mean every word I say." She spaced out the words. "Decimus—is—going—to—kill—me."

"That makes no sense." His face hardened.

"Won't you listen?" she cried. "I'm telling you the truth. He's going to have me poisoned."

"Why?" her father demands. "Camilla, this is a mad accusation."

"I'm not mad." She spoke steadily. "He's gone to Ostia to pick up a new slave, a slave who carries a satchel full of poisons." She looked at her father, seeking belief. "Didn't the trial tell you anything? Didn't you listen? Decimus is greedy. He loves money. He wants my money, all of it."

"But if he loves you—"

"Loves me?" Her voice shook. "Let me tell you how much he loves me, Papa. Decimus has never touched me, never kissed me, never, in all the years we've been married."

She looked up into her father's darkly frowning face. "Let me tell you about Decimus's loves, Papa. You will have heard about men like him. He loves little boys. He buys them. He likes twins best."

"Camilla!" her father thundered.

"You don't like to hear it, do you? I know that. But, for once in your life, I want you to know the truth. Decimus loves little boys—and Cornelia's husband."

Her father stared at her, his eyes stricken, his mouth trembling.

"That is only a little bit of the truth about Titus, Papa. I can tell you more. I can tell you why Cornelia has such a dreadful name. Did you know Titus gave her to the Emperor?"

"Silence!" he thundered. "Stop repeating your lies."

"Every word I've spoken is true." She met his angry gaze with determination. "Decimus took me to the Palace one night because he knew the Emperor liked Cornelia so well. The Emperor likes to have sisters. He made me come up to the front of the banqueting hall and he would have taken me to his bedroom, but I was so frightened I fainted. Cornelia ran up to the Emperor's table and told him I had fits. She told him that to protect me and then she went off with him."

His face crumpled. "I can't hear any more of this."

"Do I sicken you? Or do my words sicken you? Are you going to pretend now that I've never told you?"

"You are not to talk to me in such a voice!" he shouted.

She looked at him sadly. "You don't want to hear the truth because it's ugly. But I'm going to tell you the truth. All of it. Some of it isn't ugly at all. I want to tell you about myself and Marcus."

His eyes narrowed.

"You will say that I'm bad, but I don't care because I know it isn't true. I never knew a man until Marcus. I love him."

Her father's face congealed in lines of bitterness and disgust. "So that's it. You've betrayed Decimus, become a wanton."

"Is it wanton, Papa, to give yourself to the man who holds

your heart, to give yourself to a man who is in every way admirable?"

"There is nothing admirable in stealing another man's wife."

"Don't you understand yet? I was never Decimus's wife. Never!"

"A woman should attract her husband," he said stubbornly.

"Should she? But I'm not a boy, Papa."

His hand whipped through the air and caught her squarely on the cheek.

Camilla stumbled backward, her cheek flaming, but the pain from the blow couldn't match the pain in her heart.

"So I have two daughters who are whores," he said hoarsely.

"Papa." Tears glistened in Camilla's eyes. "Please. Don't you understand?"

"I understand. You're both no better than dogs in heat. If a man doesn't know his wife, she should remain chaste. As for Cornelia, she could refuse to be used—though I don't believe your story. It's just the kind of lie a woman would weave to excuse herself."

"Is it?" Camilla demanded. "My sister. My poor sister who values her sons more than anything in the world. Titus warned her that if she refused the Emperor, she'd never see her sons again."

"To barter your body for any reason is an offense," her father retorted.

"It's easy for you to judge, isn't it?" she asked bitterly. "You who've never known ugliness and treachery, yet you can judge us. Haven't you heard anything I've told you?"

"I've heard," he said brokenly. "I've heard your clever words. But I can see through innuendo and lies. I'm still orator enough for that. But I see the point of it all. You and that handsome young man. I'll see that he's disgraced."

"Papa, no!"

"I'll stop your lying with him if it's the last thing I ever do."

"You won't have to stop it. I'll be dead if you won't let me divorce Decimus."

Her words hung in the air between them.

He stared at her, his eyes hard, his mouth tight.

"Dead," she repeated. "Dead by poison."

"In the old days," he said huskily, "a husband could sentence his wife to death for adultery. If he didn't do it, her father could do so."

Her lips trembled. "I'm not a great orator, but I don't understand how you can call me an adulteress—when I've only loved one man."

"He is not your husband."

Camilla turned and walked away. At the steps, she paused and looked back. "I would ask you to do one thing for me."

The dark face stared at her emptily.

"There are twin slaves, Alexander and Ajax, two little boys Decimus used. He has new twins now and he wants to sell the little Greek boys. I'd like you to buy them and be kind to them, for they tried to help me."

She walked up the steps, leaving the green and lovely courtyard where she'd played as a little girl. Once, she nursed a wounded pigeon back to health. Behind the main fountain, she and Cornelia had played at dice. Beneath the honeysuckle arbor, she'd read, dreaming away silky summery days, looking ahead to love and marriage. She remembered her mother's gentle voice, "Do what is right, Camilla, and good will come to you." She remembered her father's voice saying, "My dear, dear daughter."

Now her father's voice remained silent. She knew he watched her climb the steps. He didn't call out.

Camilla hoped until she was in her litter. Her father's door remained closed. When Felix leaned down for instruction, she ordered, "Take me to the Campus Martius."

She went to the Temple of Jupiter and walked for a long time along the paintings and statuary. She stopped in front of a gilded statue of Adonis. She'd faced death not long ago and Marcus had saved her. This time he couldn't save her without endangering himself. Camilla knew he'd rescue her if she told him. He would kill Decimus to save her but that would spell his death.

She couldn't denounce Decimus. She mustn't let Marcus know, no matter how frightened and desperate she felt. She must solve this greatest crisis of her life alone.

She would leave Rome before Decimus and his new slave returned.

Could she see Marcus and deceive him, pretend all was well?

Camilla knew that somehow she would manage to hide her fear. She couldn't bear to leave Rome without seeing—and loving—Marcus one last time.

XVI

Marcus stretched out his hands.

Camilla grasped them and delighted in their warmth and strength. "Marcus," she said softly. She looked at him, trying to imprint on her mind and heart for all time, for the last time, the dear lines of his face, dark eyes that glinted with humor and kindness and love, thick dark curly hair and bold nose, full lips and blunt chin.

He gazed at her intently. "I've been thinking about you all morning." A shadow touched his eyes. "I have a feeling that something's wrong. You know how the air grows cold when the sun slips behind a cloud? This morning, early, I was thinking of you." He smiled a little, almost impishly, "I think of you every day. In every way." His frown returned. "This morning I was thinking of you and suddenly, it was like taking an unexpected step in the dark or losing your way. I was frightened." He stared down at her, perplexed. "You seem all right."

"I'm fine," she said quickly. She made her voice firm and strong. Before he could say more, ask again, she reached up and locked her hands behind his head and drew his face down and kissed him.

"Hmm," he murmured, "now that's the way to begin an afternoon."

She laughed softly. "You and I know how to spend our afternoons, don't we?"

Delighted, he swept her up in his arms and strode to the bedroom. He swung Camilla to her feet beside his bed. His hands cupped her shoulders. "You're more beautiful every day. How can I be so lucky to be the man who possesses you?"

"Because you're Marcus," she said quietly. "You are the love of my life. I admire you more than any man I've ever known."

Marcus's face sobered. "Do you mean that?"

"Yes. I do."

"As much as you admire your father?"

"More." Her answer came sharply, convincingly. She paused and swallowed. "You would never be cruel."

"No one could be cruel to you, Camilla."

She slipped her fingers up into his hair. "I love the feel of your hair, your skin. I love the way you touch me, the way you make me feel. Marcus, I want to love you completely."

His eyes burned into hers. They stood so close. They knew each other, knew love, its pulse and feel and race. Expectation merged with anticipation to fuel the exquisite knowledge of what was to come.

Marcus touched her throat then his hand slipped down to loosen her gown. She stepped out of her tunic and he shrugged free from his heavy toga. Marcus took her hand and pulled her down to the bed. They faced each other, their limbs gleaming like ivory in the soft dusky light of the shuttered room.

They came together and she rejoiced in the feel of his body next to hers. Camilla's hands slipped up his back. She looked into his face, so near hers. She wanted to tell him how much she cared, how much she thanked the gods for him and for the love they'd known, for every precious moment, the tenderness and the passion and the delight. But this was denied her because then he'd know his fear was true, that indeed something was terribly wrong.

"Marcus," she said quietly, "the gods are jealous of us."

"Perhaps that's why we can't marry now," he agreed. "But we can still love."

She dropped her gaze. He didn't know how jealous the gods were. She couldn't tell him.

Tenderly, Camilla's mouth touched his, lightly, gently, sweetly.

"Camilla, Camilla," he said softly, his mouth moving beneath hers.

She kissed him passionately, desperately, hungrily. His hands touched her and desire exploded between them and they came together in a surge of ecstasy that nothing in the world could rival, a sweep of pure delight, complete, perfect, and sublime.

When they lay quietly in the enchanted circle of each other's arms, their faces so near, still bemused by the power of their love, Marcus said huskily, "It's going to come right, Camilla. I know it will. I've no doubt at all."

Camilla closed her eyes briefly, but somewhere deep within found the strength to open them and look into his eyes. "I love you," she said simply. That was all she said.

He smiled hugely. "You and I, Camilla. Our love was ordained in the stars."

"I love you, Marcus."

When they were dressed and walking slowly toward the door, hand in hand, Marcus said happily, "There's no court tomorrow. I have the whole day free. Let's have a picnic, then go to a concert."

Camilla's heart ached inside, raging and twisting like a wounded animal, but she smiled brightly. "That would be such fun."

He walked downstairs with her and stood in the doorway of the shop, smiling farewell, confident and happy, sure of her and their future.

Camilla waved once, closed the curtains of her litter, and lay back against the silk cushions.

"Goodbye."

Her lips silently formed the words: *goodbye, farewell, the gods be with you, Marcus.*

When she reached the house, she climbed from the litter, drained but composed. She hurried into the reception hall and said sharply to a young slave. "Find Phoebe. And Priscus. Immediately."

Camilla paced up and down by the shimmering pool.

Phoebe hurried to her. "Yes, mistress."

"Order the carriages packed at once to go to Swallow's Nest."

"Today?" Phoebe asked in surprise.

"This very instant. Pack what I will need for a week's stay."

Priscus came forward, frowning. "The master said nothing about your going to Swallow's Nest."

"No," Camilla retorted. "He didn't. But I am going. You may tell your master when he returns with his new slave."

Did Priscus's face flatten just a little? Did he, too, know?

"Help Phoebe prepare for the trip," Camilla ordered. "I wish to leave within the hour."

Camilla turned and walked down into the courtyard, but the gracious surroundings felt alien. She had no desire to walk up into the parkland. The memory of being there with Marcus was overlaid, stained, by the thin high whispers of the little boys. She walked up and down the courtyard paths. She was in a hurry to leave. She would have at least a few days of safety at Swallow's Nest and she would be where she'd spent the happiest weeks of her life, the wonderful weeks when she and Marcus explored the glories of love, when they spread his cloak across the dusty cave floor and listened to the soft slap of sea water and shared exquisite pleasure.

She would find some way to survive. Somehow, she would best Decimus in this battle he had joined.

When the litters were ready, Camilla stopped in the library. She opened a wax tablet, slowly and carefully began to write.

My dearest Marcus,

I'm so sorry I can't come tomorrow for our picnic. I must, very unexpectedly, leave for Swallow's Nest. Do miss me. I'll soon return and, once again, we'll share our afternoons.

Love,
Camilla

She touched the tiny little ridges in the wax that spelled his name, snapped the tablet shut, wrapped twine about it, and sealed it. She carried the tablet with her out to the front steps.

"Your litter is ready," Phoebe said, breathlessly. "But it's late afternoon now. Why don't you wait and get a good start in the morning?"

"I want to leave now. Phoebe, you are to deliver this message for me, then you may come catch up with us."

She gave Phoebe careful directions on how to find Marcus' apartment. "This letter is very important. Do just as I tell you."

Phoebe nodded.

Camilla's last glimpse of the house in Rome was of Phoebe standing outside the entry, holding the tablet in her gnarled hands, her face drawn with concern.

Camilla lay back in her litter as they left Rome and stared

dry-eyed at the dusty countryside. Throughout the next four days, on the road or during her restless sleep at friends' villas, her mind struggled, thoughts darting like frightened mice twisting and turning to escape a cat's paw.

How could she escape the poisoner's hand?

She could be careful what she ate, eating only what others tasted first.

But at one meal or another, this day or that, the potion would slip past her and death would come.

Could she seek sanctuary with Cornelia? Titus was Decimus's lover. There could be no safety there.

She could travel. Visit Aunt Lollia in Pompeii.

A hefty bribe could open a kitchen to gloved hands.

On the last day of her journey, Camilla moved restlessly in her litter. She'd thought and schemed and prayed but no solution had come. Her hours were running out just as surely as sand slips from the top of an hourglass, silently and swiftly. As they rounded a curve, she saw the gleaming façade of the villa that belonged to her father's old friend, Tiberius Capito. Tiberius had loved her since she was a little girl. Camilla gestured for the train to stop.

Felix hurried to her side. "We're almost there, my lady."

"I wish to leave a message at Tiberius Capito's villa."

The slave nodded.

"Bring me a wax tablet and a stylus. Quickly."

When she held the tablet in her lap, Camilla frowned thoughtfully, then, hand flying, she impressed letters on the soft wax. When she was finished, she read the message and nodded in satisfaction.

"Send the rest of the train ahead, Felix, but take me to the Capito villa."

Tiberius welcomed her with a shout. "Come in and have a cool glass of wine, Camilla. Tell me about your journey."

"I'd love to." She climbed down from her litter then turned

to Felix. "Go ahead to Swallow's Nest. I'll walk home by the sea path."

When she and Tiberius were alone, Camilla slipped her arm through his. "Will you walk with me for a moment?"

"Camilla, it will be an honor and delight to walk with you." He beamed at her, his lined face filled with kindness.

She smiled up at him and felt a rush of affection. Dear Tiberius. He had brought little presents to her and her sisters when they were children, encouraged them in their studies, revered them as his best friend's daughters. And now, though he wouldn't know it, she hoped he would be her rescuer.

As they climbed toward the cliff, Camilla said, "Tiberius, I'd like to ask a very great favor of you."

He looked down, surprised at her serious tone. He replied in kind. "Of course, my dear. If I can be of any service to you, please tell me."

She held out the tablet, sealed with wax. "I'd like you to keep this for me. Should anything happen to me, should I become ill and die, I'd like you to open it and read it."

He frowned. "You're only a slip of a girl and I'm an old man. You'll live years longer than I."

"Sometimes," she said slowly, "evil chance touches our lives."

His frown deepened. "Camilla, what's wrong?"

She looked at him gravely. "I can't say more. But it would give me very great peace of mind if you promise to do as I ask."

He tucked the tablet under one arm and took her hands in his. "I promise. But surely you know that if you need me, I'm always at your call."

She smiled and kissed his cheek. "Thank you, dear Tiberius, thank you so much. Now, I must go home. But we will visit one day soon."

When she reached the turn in the path, she saw Tiberius standing where she'd left him, holding the tablet and staring after her.

Rounding the curve, the sharp wind pressed against her. She welcomed the chill, felt her blood pounding in concert with the sea. The sea spread purplish dark to the faraway horizon. Spume glittered as waves crashed against the rocky shore.

Camilla followed the path that skirted the headlands and led to the rocky point where she'd first seen Marcus. Camilla clambered to the top point and looked out at the roiling waters.

"Camilla."

She heard his shout and knew him at once, yet turned in disbelief. He called again and she saw him running up the path toward her, his arms outstretched.

"Marcus," she cried wonderingly, and she came into his embrace with a surge of happiness.

He touched his mouth against her hair. "I got your message. I know I should have stayed in Rome, but I got a delay on some cases and came as soon as I could. I tried hard to catch you along the way. I couldn't bear to be separated from you for even a week." He held her tightly. "A day is too long."

She clung to him, her face buried against his chest.

He laughed. "You missed me, too, didn't you?"

Camilla smiled into his eyes. The joy of being with him once again, so unexpectedly, made the afternoon a gift from the gods. She touched his cheek.

"I never thought you'd come," she said softly.

"I don't want to be away from you. I'd follow you to the ends of the earth."

Her lips half opened. She wanted, desperately, to ask him to run away with her. Perhaps if they went to the ends of the world they would be safe, but she knew the answer to that and she was not going to put him in danger. He was here, now, this moment. This moment could be theirs, forever.

"Let's go down to our cave, Marcus."

"Let's." He took her hand.

She laughed aloud as they struggled down the twisting path, almost blown off into the sea by the gusting wind.

"September's a better month for lovers at the shore." He had to shout for her to hear above the wind and the crash of the waves.

"I don't mind the wind," she shouted back.

They burst into the cave and came up against each other in the startling quiet.

Camilla kissed his face with tiny, swift kisses, delicate as a whirling wisp of fog in December. He stood very still, his hands clasping her waist, his dark eyes watching her tenderly. Her lips found his and they kissed long and lingeringly and the wonderful sweet passion mounted within them.

They shrugged out of their clothes, her gown and his tunic slipping to the dusty floor. Marcus lifted her in his arms and buried his face against her breasts. Camilla touched the wonderfully strong muscles on his shoulders and back. Slowly, they sank to the cave floor. Their lips met again, Marcus' hands slipped down to touch her thighs, and Camilla exploded with desire.

They came together and the moment seemed to stretch and grow like sunlight captured in a prism, brilliant, fiery, almost unendurable.

"Camilla, my love," he said softly when passion was spent.

"My love," she responded.

Then it was time to leave their magic place of love. The wind was harder now, the salt sea spray icy, as they struggled up the path. At the top, Marcus took her hand.

"You look a little crumpled," he said ruefully. He straightened the line of her gown. In passing, his hand touched her breast.

Camilla smiled. "I don't care. I'd rather be crumpled from loving you than wear the finest gown in Rome."

"We'll have a picnic tomorrow," he said happily. "We'll walk for miles. Miles and miles."

"Tomorrow," she said, smiling.

She left him standing on the high point. She stopped once to look back and the late afternoon sun burnished him with gold. Her breath caught in her chest. It was so like the very first time she'd glimpsed him. She lifted her hand and waved. How comforting to know that he would be at his villa. Yet, she felt a shift within, she must break off their meetings, persuade him to return to Rome, keep him safe. But perhaps they could have this week together.

Camilla was smiling as she followed the twisting path along the wind-stunted pines. Marcus was here and she was here. And she'd made herself safe for now. She was still smiling as she rounded a curve, then she stumbled to a stop, her face blank. She shaded her eyes against the blood red rays of the setting sun, but there was no mistaking that lean figure coming toward her.

Camilla's heart began to thud.

"I didn't know you were here," she said thinly.

Decimus nodded and a slight smile touched his sensual mouth. "I arrived last night. Isn't it a lovely chance that we both should come to Swallow's Nest." He stepped nearer. "Shall we walk for a moment before dinner, Camilla. Work up an appetite?" She saw the darkness in his eyes and knew death awaited her at dinner.

"Yes," she said forcefully. "Let's walk back this way. I must talk to you."

He looked puzzled at her tone, then gave a little shrug and

followed as she turned and started down the path. She walked quickly, following the twisting trail, back to the top of bluff.

She loved being here in the whipping wind, high about the buffeting water. It was here she'd first seen Marcus. It was from here that he had come to her rescue after her fall. She felt a surge of courage when she turned to face Decimus.

She stared at him for a moment, said bluntly, "I understand you've bought a new slave."

His faun-like face might have been carved in stone. Then he nodded carelessly, "That's right." He smiled, an inward, knowing smile. "He's good at problem solving."

Camilla didn't hesitate. The letter she'd left with Tiberius was an amulet to protect her. She said coolly, "With poisons?"

His eyes were as cold as death. They stood in a pocket of silence amid the boom of the surf and the keening of the wind.

She looked into his dark and icy eyes and a wave of horror touched her. "I know what you planned, Decimus." Once before she'd forced him to her will. She felt confident with Tiberius as her protector that she could now defeat Decimus.

He took a step toward her.

She held up her hand. "You won't get away with killing me. You'll be tried for murder if you poison me."

"Why should that be?" he asked huskily.

"I've left a message with a friend. If I fall sick and die, he's promised to open the tablet and read it."

Decimus poked his head forward. "What did you write?"

She wished she could see him more clearly, but his face was a dull blur in the dusk. The tone in his voice chilled her, but he wouldn't dare have her poisoned now. If he did, Tiberius would bring a charge of murder against him.

"I wrote that you hired a slave skilled in poisons and you

intended to have him poison me so you could inherit all of my land and money."

The silence between them pulsed with his anger.

"That was clever of you. But not quite clever enough."

Camilla started to step back from him. Then she realized she stood almost at the edge of the cliff. Behind her the ground fell sharply away and below the sea pounded against the rocks.

"There's nothing you can do," she said loudly.

"I can't have you poisoned," he said casually, as if discussing the weather or wheat prices. "But since you've been good enough to tell me about the letter, I'll take advantage of it."

She felt a quiver of uncertainty. "Advantage?"

He nodded. "I've told several of our friends how concerned I've been about you lately. These odd mood changes. The letter will be even more proof that you haven't been yourself."

That was what her father had said. "You aren't yourself, Camilla."

"Don't you understand?" she demanded. "I've put a stop to your scheme."

He ignored her. "Several of our friends have noticed your melancholy. Titus and I talked about it the other day. And there's your earlier attempt to end everything by flinging yourself into the water. The letter will be certain evidence you were unhinged."

"There's nothing wrong with my mind," she said sharply. "I'll tell everyone what you've said."

He laughed aloud. "Don't you understand? You won't be here to tell anyone anything."

He lunged for her.

She tried to slip past him, but he grabbed her. As she struggled, Decimus clapped his hand over her mouth to stifle her scream. One arm swept her up. "I'll be devastated," he said jerkily as he fought her toward the edge of the cliff, "when your body washes up. Your tragic death will go down as an accident, but some will whisper about suicide."

Camilla writhed and twisted, heart pounding, terror pulsing through her.

His fingers dug into her arms. He held her with ferocious strength.

She kicked at his leg but he laughed, swinging her up. With a heave, he flung her over the edge of the precipice.

Plummeting down and down and down, she struggled to breathe. It seemed forever and then she struck with sickening force, sinking into the icy, cold, enveloping, killing water. The folds of her sodden cloak were heavy as chains. She plunged deeper and deeper into the dark water where death would claim her. This time Marcus would not be here to save her. Choking, gasping, struggling against the fiery pain in her throat and lungs, she tried to shed her cloak. But she knew her fingers were feeble, slipping away, unable to grasp the cloth. Blackness swept into her mind . . .

Suddenly strong hands gripped her arms and she began to rise in the water. No, she thought dimly, that was the time before when Marcus saved her. Not this time.

"Camilla!"

The urgent, demanding shout pierced the blackness, drew her back. "Camilla!"

She felt a tremendous blow against her back. Air swept her face. Choking and heaving and gasping, air reached her starving lungs. She looked dazedly about and realized she was hanging over Marcus's shoulder in the roiling water and he was pounding on her back.

"Marcus," she cried weakly.

"Camilla!" He shouted her name in triumph. "I was afraid I was too late. I saw him. I'll kill him, I swear it. He threw you over the cliff."

It was hard to speak, to find breath for words and her voice was as weak as the faraway sound of a dove. "How did you see?"

"After you left, I decided to swim. I think of you when I dive from the cliff and so I went down into the water. I swam out to the head and was returning to shore. I looked up and saw you on the cliff, you and Decimus."

"The water's so rough . . ."

Even now waves slapped against them and only the strength of his legs kept them afloat.

Marcus grinned. "These waves aren't my match. Especially not tonight." His voice hardened. "I was swimming back to shore. I saw him throw you over the cliff to die."

"You came," she said softly. Tears burned in her eyes. "I needed you and you came."

"I'll always come. No matter where you are or what happens, Camilla, I'll be there."

A wave crashed over them. As Camilla sputtered, he pulled her close. "We'll go in now. I'll see to Decimus."

He helped her shed the heavy cloak. He stroked and pulled them steadily nearer the cliff face. Then, gauging the crash of the waves, he brought them onto the rocks and safely to land.

Once on the path, Camilla stood unsteadily, supported by his hand. She shivered against the wet coldness of her gown which clung to her. Camilla looked up at him. "You mustn't accuse Decimus. He'll kill us both."

"I'll see to Decimus," he said again, his voice stern. He picked her up and started up the cliff path.

"No," she cried. "It's too dangerous for you."

Marcus only tightened his grip and thrust his head forward and walked more swiftly.

When they reached the villa, he pushed through the door with his foot and looked warily around the entrance hall.

Then, clearly on the still night air, they heard Decimus speaking. His voice carried very clearly. "Father Scipio, I hardly know what to tell you. Camilla hasn't been herself for several months now. She has odd fancies. I'm quite concerned about her. Tonight, I understand she arrived here and got out of her litter before she even reached the villa and struck off toward the cliff path, muttering to herself and looking quite wild. I believe we should send out a search party. I was getting ready to do so when you arrived."

Camilla pressed Marcus's arm. He helped her stand. She took a weak step or two toward the voices, gathered more strength, continued forward, head high despite the drenched dress that clung to her. She stopped at the top of the courtyard steps and called out, "I'm here, Decimus." She spoke gravely as she looked at the lean man she'd once thought handsome, the man who had planned to kill her, who would rejoice at her death, the man who was lying to her father.

As Decimus jumped up from the table, his wine goblet crashed to the pavement. He whirled and stared through the dim light of early dusk. Fear blanched his face. "You're dead." His voice was high, unsteady, terrified. "I threw you down to the sea. Go away. You're dead." The last was almost a scream.

Camilla took one step, another, unsteady, water streaming from her gown, her face a pale oval in the dim light.

Camilla's father jumped to his feet, turned toward Decimus. His patrician face twisted in pain. "What are you saying, Decimus? Camilla dead?"

Decimus stepped backward, hands held up to ward off a

phantom. "I threw her from the cliff. She's come back to haunt me."

Camilla's father drew a short knife from his toga, moved inexorably toward Decimus. "Camilla told me you were going to kill her. I didn't believe her. But her words stayed in my mind and my heart and I came as fast as I could."

Camilla broke into a run and reached her father to grab his upraised arm.

"Papa, no, Marcus was swimming by the point and he saw Decimus throw me and he saved me. I'm here."

The knife clattered to the floor. Her father pulled her close. "My girl, my cherished daughter, forgive me. You came to me and I sent you away." His voice broke.

"But you came tonight."

Tears streamed down his face. "My heart told me I was a fool. I listened finally and I came as fast as I could. Will you forgive me?"

She touched his wet cheek. "You will always be my hero, Papa."

"No." Her father was abrupt. "Here is our hero." He turned to Marcus. "You saved my daughter again."

Marcus came up beside Camilla. "Yes." His voice was strong. "I've saved her twice. Now I will ask you to repay me."

Her father nodded slowly. "I owe you so much. I can never be out of your debt."

"You can acquit your debt. Give me Camilla to be my wife."

Her father looked at her, tears in his eyes. "Camilla, I traveled as hard as I could. I came because even though my mind rejected your calm, my heart believed. You told the truth."

"Yes, Papa. I told the truth."

He nodded and turned toward Decimus and looked at him with loathing. "You are evil and you almost destroyed my daughter. But I won't bring charges. Instead, I demand her divorce from you." He looked at Camilla. "And I'm going to demand a divorce for Cornelia when I return to Rome. Titus won't hold back my grandsons, not if he wants to keep even a penny of Cornelia's dowry. Cornelia can be free of the ugliness that has pulled at her, free to enjoy her sons, free perhaps to find love."

Camilla threw her arms around her father. Tears streamed down her face.

He looked down, smiling at her through his own tears. Then he disengaged her arms and turned her toward Marcus. He looked fully at Marcus. "You are a good man, an honorable man, the man my daughter deserves as her husband. She will now be yours. May the gods bless your union, may you walk in sunshine."

ABOUT THE AUTHOR

Carolyn Hart, an accomplished master of mystery, is the author of twenty previous Death on Demand novels. Her books have won multiple Agatha, Anthony, and Macavity Awards. She is also the creator of the Henrie O series which features a retired reporter, and the Bailey Ruth series which stars an impetuous, redheaded ghost. One of the founders of Sisters in Crime, Hart lives in Oklahoma City.

CAROLYN HART CLASSICS

FROM OPEN ROAD MEDIA

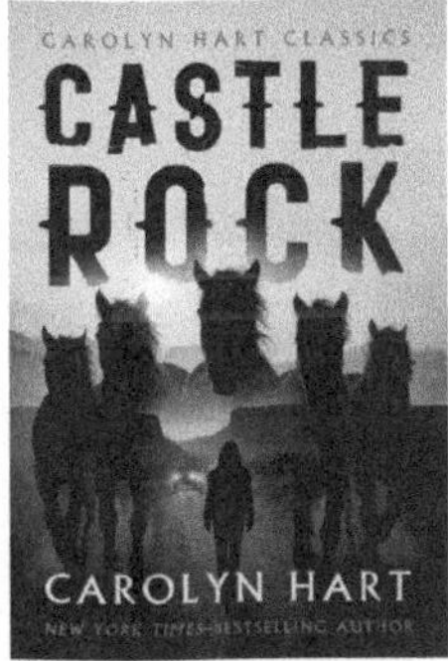

Find a full list of our authors and titles at www.openroadmedia.com

FOLLOW US
@OpenRoadMedia

EARLY BIRD BOOKS
FRESH DEALS, DELIVERED DAILY

Love to read?
Love great sales?

Get fantastic deals on bestselling ebooks delivered to your inbox every day!

Sign up today at
earlybirdbooks.com/book